Four Days Outside of Del Norte

A Western Frontier Adventure

Robert Peecher

For information the author may be contacted at

PO Box 967; Watkinsville GA; 30677

or at mooncalfpress.com

This is a work of fiction. Any similarities to actual events in whole or in part are purely accidental. None of the characters or events depicted in this novel are intended to represent actual people.

FOR JEAN

- 1 -

From behind a rocky outcropping, and hidden by the branches of a thick cedar tree, Jacob Stallings watched the small party of prospectors on the trail down below him. Like a mountain river, the road cut a path through the valley, fed by trails that dropped down from the peaks to the west, the north, and the south. The trails cut into the newly opened San Juan mountains, available to prospectors with the signing of a treaty with the Ute. The road to the east led to Del Norte, the small town from which the prospectors had begun their journey into the mountains in the spring, and the town they returned to now to sit out the winter.

They were eight men down on the road, afoot and each one leading a pack mule. Their party consisted of rugged men, survivors accustomed to hardship. They would not lie down easily. But surprise and overwhelming numbers could do much against even hardy men.

Those pack mules were loaded with supplies, but at least a couple of them also toted quantities of gold ore that would make Jacob Stallings a very wealthy man.

Jacob took a deep breath and shifted his grip on the hatchet in his hand. The moment was now. The hatchet was the only artifice he needed. Some had suggested they wear buckskins or feathers or paint their faces, but none of that was necessary. The hatchet Jacob Stallings held and the similar weapons his men carried, they would pull off the illusion of an Indian attack. He glanced across at his brother Lou and gave him a nod. Lou, also hidden behind a thick cedar, nodded back.

Quietly, Lou rose up from his crouched position and started forward down the slope. Other men, equally hidden and poised, followed Lou's example. Jacob Stallings waited a moment to allow the others time to get started down the hill. They would be the better men for this job. Ambush and murder were not Jacob Stallings' specialty, but his outfit was manned by those who did specialize in murder. Including the two Stallings brothers, there were twenty-four men in the outfit. They would easily and quickly overtake eight unsuspecting prospectors.

The two dozen men descended the slope several yards, and then Lou gave a shout, and now they went down in a rush.

From his tardy position on the hill, Jacob Stallings had a view of the onslaught.

Lou and the others dashed down the hill, so fast that one among them lost his feet and tumbled head over heels.

They shouted as they went, their prehistoric weapons raised up high in the air. Lou and the others, they caught out those prospectors leading their mules – caught them out completely unawares, completely unprepared.

One of them had a six-gun that he tried to wrest free from its holster, but Lou was on him. Lou, toting a heavy club, brained him with one swing of the club. Lou's thick arm swung that heavy club, all the momentum from his run down the slope combining with all his weight behind the swing. That prospector's head smashed open like a watermelon.

Lou and the others shouted and murdered as they fell in among the prospectors, and they made short work of it. Jacob Stallings reflected that surprise and speed were gruesome to witness.

Lou and the others struck in ghastly violence, knives and spears and hatchets going to work on the small party of prospectors. They struck so fast and with such complete surprise that none among the prospectors had time to properly defend themselves.

Jacob Stallings now followed into the horror.

One of the prospectors, a thick-bearded man with wide shoulders, had his back to Jacob Stallings and with a big-bladed fighting knife was facing off one of Stallings' men. Stallings locked his eyes on those big shoulders as he dashed down the slope. He raised up his hatchet and brought it down hard between those big shoulders. The heavy prospector crumpled to his knees. Stallings wrenched the hatchet free and swung down again, splitting the man's skull.

And that was it, the final blow that had to be struck. The work was done in a jiffy.

The surprise had been complete. Not a man in Stallings' group suffered a wound other than Nicolas Schimmel who took a musket butt to the jaw.

A few of the men in the Stallings outfit set to work collecting scalps from the prospectors, but this was all they took. Jacob Stallings had been adamant. No theft, not any at all. They would get shed of the scalps as soon as they found a good spot. And then there would be nothing to tie Stallings and his men to these murders. No engraved pocket watch. No embroidered shot pouch. No lucky rabbits foot. Nothing could be lifted from the bodies except their scalps.

They killed the mules, too, and that was worse than killing the men. The mules screeched and bellowed and their sounds echoed off the cliffs beyond the river. Jacob Stallings did not participate in the slaughtering of the animals. He would have preferred that it be done with muskets over knives and spears, but here they had to continue the artifice.

Primitive weapons – spears and hatchets and clubs and knives. In the coming days – hell, in the coming hours – prospectors heading in for the winter would cross this scene of slaughter. And they would all tell the same story down below.

A band of prospectors along the Rio Grande trail in the San Juan Mountains, about four days' walk outside of Del Norte, were killed by Injuns. That's the story they would tell.

Jacob Stallings found the ore in a pannier on one of the murdered beasts. He looked at it, and just on sight he could tell that it was as good as he'd been told. But he resisted the temptation to take any of it. The gold would make him rich, but not by taking this gold.

- 2 -

The snow covered the horses' fetlocks with each step.

In the cold stillness of the mountain trail, the repeating soft crunch of snow collapsing under hoof sounded out its melancholy song.

Sometimes a man in the column would cough or sniffle, or a horse might snort, or a saber rattle. The drooping branches of the pines somewhere deep in the forest would sometimes give way under the weight of ice and collected snow, and with a snap and a crash, the falling branch would remind the men that they existed on a world bigger than just the saddle, the next step.

But when the horses did not snort or a man did not cough or a branch did not give, just the soft crunch of hoofs packing snow was all the men heard.

A quiet and cold place, rocky cliffs, hills thick with fir, cedar and pine, and sometimes, when the trail dropped low, the constant sound of the stream rolling over its rocky bed, too early yet to freeze. The snow was a prelude. If the clouds would blow out, the afternoon would warm up and the sun would likely melt off most of the snow. In two weeks or three, but sooner than a month, this snow would be the way of things until the spring. This cold snap came early, unseasonal, but soon the cold and snow would come in earnest.

Ten riders in their government issues, three pack mules. They moved slow. The cold seemed to slow everything. The horses trod with less enthusiasm. The riders had no energy to push harder.

They struck out before sunup, though the sun never really shone. Not here. Not today. The gray sky lightened, but the clouds hung like a thick covering and blocked out any warmth the sun might give.

The column of cavalrymen left out of Fort Garland a week before with provisions enough for a short campaign into the mountains west of the new town. Del Norte, they called it. Prospectors coming into the town out of the mountains brought news of a massacre along the banks of the Rio Grande on the trail down from the mining camps, the sort of massacre the soldiers at Fort Garland were meant to prevent.

A band of Utes hadn't taken kindly to the opening of the San Juan mountains.

It fell to Lieutenant Elliot Turner to lead the column. Two years out of West Point, with an uncle who had distinguished himself in the war, Turner greeted news of the command with enthusiasm. A young man full of theory, he had prayed daily for the opportunity to wrap himself in glory.

"This is a march for appearances," the colonel had said. "You won't find the Utes, and as you get up higher, you'll find the snow has already started. But the prospectors coming down from the mountain need to see the army making some move. Investigate the site of the massacre. Bury anything left to bury. Scout around the hills. Then return to the fort."

They were now four days outside Del Norte, and somewhere not far up ahead they would find the site of the killing. They'd passed a group of prospectors leading mules down out of the mountains who had seen the site.

Up ahead, out of sight, the cavalry's scout likely had already reached the site.

Levi Stout remained an enigma to the West Point graduate.

Since he'd first arrived at Fort Garland, Lieutenant Turner had made several attempts to get to know Stout. The man had served a decade as a scout. He'd been with the Pawnee scouts during campaigns against the Sioux in Wyoming and the Dakotas. They said he'd covered more ground in Colorado Territory than anyone in the army and more than most prospectors. He had no official capacity in the army at present, but he'd taken up with a Mexican widow in San Luis and often came to Fort Garland in search of work. Most of that work these days entailed running dispatches, either to Santa Fe or Fort Union. But Stout had arrived at Fort Garland the same evening that word came in of a massacre in the mountains west of Del Norte, and he'd agreed to lead Lieutenant Turner's expedition.

Still, though he led the command to which Stout was presently attached, Lieutenant Turner had been unable to get more than a few words out of the man.

The falling snow began to whisper in the gray silence of the morning, speaking softly as it landed on the brims of their hats, the shoulders of their coats, the manes of the horses. It fell heavy and thick so that the men could see very little in front of them.

Sergeant O'Keefe, a wiry Irishman who'd seen combat in the war and decided anyway to make a career of the army, stepped his horse up the column to reach the lieutenant.

"Conditions are getting worse," he said. "We should do what we can at the site of the massacre and then think about heading back down, if ya like."

Lieutenant Turner grunted a noncommittal response. He would not be cowed by weather or fear of Ute attack. He'd objected mildly to his orders – a campaign for appearances, the colonel had called it. To Lieutenant Turner, it made no sense to send a column of cavalry into the mountains just to ease the minds of prospectors. Either they were going to locate the Utes responsible for the attack or they ought not go at all.

The sergeant waited, eager to hear some word from the lieutenant that might suggest they would be turning around after they'd buried the remains of the party attacked by the Utes. But the lieutenant offered no such guarantees, and eventually the sergeant reined up and allowed the column to pass him.

One of the privates, also an Irishman and veteran of the war and therefore a man more like a brother than a subordinate to O'Keefe, stepped his horse over close to the sergeant.

"Press into the mountains is it, then?" the private said.

"Looks to be," O'Keefe said. "We'll be frozen before we get back to the fort."

***

Levi Stout, kneeling close to the ground, swept the snow away with his forearm and then lightly brushed what remained with his gloved hand.

He'd been hours searching, but now at last he'd discovered the place where they'd held the horses. It was high up, beyond a ridge and out of sight from the trail below, as he suspected it would be. Despite the snow, the tracks in the ground were still discernible. When the ambush had taken place, almost ten days ago, now, there'd been no snow on the ground.

Stout did all he could at the site of the massacre, though that was little enough. Probably two hundred or more prospectors had come out of the hills and along this trail in the last ten days. When word of the massacre reached Fort Garland, they'd said that the bodies had been left as they were. But someone since then had seen fit to bury the bodies. A Christian act, but one that complicated things for the cavalry's scout. Levi Stout was only able to find the graves – now covered over by snow – when he saw the stack of rifles that had been left beside the line of graves. The men who buried the bodies did not bother to dig holes. Instead, they simply dragged the bodies off the trail and then covered them over in rocks. It had been an afternoon's labor and surely delayed the party getting to

Del Norte or wherever they intended to winter.

Stout only uncovered a couple of the bodies. He found what he needed to find fast enough.

The mules were left where they fell. Gruesome work to kill the mules, done with knives and spears. They still had their packs.

Stout picked through the remains of the mules as well. The bodies of the animals, left to the elements, were covered by snow and had been disturbed by coyotes and birds and whatever else came along to scavenge, maybe even a bear or two. Looking for evidence was also gruesome work.

As best as Stout could make out, none of the prospectors who passed by the scene had molested the packs. He found a significant amount of what appeared to be gold ore. Stout had been in the Black Hills when gold was discovered there, and he knew a little bit of what he was looking at as he turned the dirty-white rocks over in his hands. The yellow streaks visible in some of the white quartz told the tale that these prospectors had found a wealthy vein.

The evidence he sought among the mules was in the packs. What was taken? What remained? That would tell a tale as well as anything.

But Levi Stout found very little to suggest that anything was taken. These prospectors came out of the hills above with gold ore, blankets and tents, shot, powder, tools, pots and pans, and even rifles – stacked over near the graves – and they'd been left for eternity with all these same possessions.

By the time Stout saw the column of blue-clad horse soldiers winding their way along the trail toward him, he'd already reached his conclusions about what had happened here, who was responsible for it, and who was not.

***

"It was white men did this," the army scout told Lieutenant Turner.

The nine men of the cavalry patrol were in the spruce trees a little ways farther up the trail setting up their camp for the night. Sergeant O'Keefe was supervising their efforts, though any one of those men was capable of pitching a tent and collecting firewood without the sergeant barking commands.

While the others of his command made camp, Levi Stout took the lieutenant around the scene. He pointed out the graves and showed the two he'd uncovered. He pointed out the rifles stacked by the graves. Showed the mules, their innards torn loose by animals and picked at by birds. All the signs and indications he'd discovered while he waited for the cavalry patrol to catch up to him, he showed to the lieutenant, except the tracks beyond the ridge. That would be a hike, and the scout did not care to go back up there again just now.

The lieutenant stood by the blood-red snow where the mules' carcasses had been mauled by wolves and every other thing. He scanned the scene and considered all that Levi Stout had pointed out to him. He'd understood that the scout was driving toward a conclusion, but even as they neared it, the lieutenant wasn't quite sure what conclusion he was supposed to arrive at. And that's when Stout at last came out with his accusation: White men, not Indians.

"The reports we had suggested it was a band of Utes," Lieutenant Turner said.

"Yes, sir," Stout allowed. "But these prospectors coming out of these hills, they see angry Utes in every shadow. They come upon something like this, and they'll say it was Indians every time. They won't dig around in the bloody snow to figure it out for themselves. They'll just see slaughter and blame it on the Utes or whatever other Indians might be around. But I'm saying I've looked it over, and this was the work of white men."

"Are there rifle shots to suggest it was white men?" Lieutenant Turner asked.

"No, sir. Clubs and spears and knives and hatchets."

"The weapons of Indians," Lieutenant Turner said. "White men would have made quick work of this with rifle shots from that hill above."

"They came off of that hill, all right," Stout said. "It was an ambush, sure enough. But it wasn't Indians."

Lieutenant Turner studied tactical maneuvers at West Point. He studied military history. He even studied about irregular warfare such as that employed by the Indians. But he learned nothing of reading the sign at the scene of a massacre such as this, nor did he have experience enough in battle to equip him to understand what he was looking at. He lacked the experience to understand what convinced Stout that this was not an ambush by Ute warriors attempting to send a message to other prospectors in these hills.

So he began to question Stout, not so much from his position as the officer in command as from a man trying to learn from one with more knowledge.

"Explain to me what you see that convinces you,"

Lieutenant Turner said.

Stout grunted in the back of his throat, and Turner wondered what the grunt meant. Had he too many times been pressed by young lieutenants to explain things that he plainly saw while they remained ignorant?

"What kind of Indian doesn't steal a gun and shot and powder?" Stout asked.

"I don't know, Mr. Stout," Lieutenant Turner responded. "Perhaps you can tell me what kind of Indian."

"No kind of Indian," Stout said flatly.

"How can you be sure? Perhaps there was another party of prospectors coming and the Indians rushed away, leaving the job incomplete. There are bands of Utes dissatisfied with the Brunot Treaty that surrendered these mountains to the United States. Perhaps they committed this massacre not to steal guns and powder but to send a message."

Stout shook his head, not doubtfully but disdainfully.

"Lieutenant, Indians ain't like white men. A white man shoots a buffalo and he takes the hide off of it and the tongue, maybe. The rest of it he leaves for the birds and the coyotes and to rot. An Indian kills a buffalo, and he takes every bit of that creature that can be used. You see? He don't do nothing to send a message. If it was Utes that done this, they'd have taken the blankets, they'd have taken the mules, they'd have taken the rifles and powder horns and the shot. Hell, the only thing they'd have left was the gold."

Lieutenant Turner nodded, almost willing to accept the scout's knowledge. He'd led his expedition into the mountains believing he was coming to the site of an Indian massacre, and it was hard to turn loose of that belief. He was not prepared to find something else here. But he had one more point to argue.

"But a white man would have taken the gold," he said.

Levi Stout grunted a response.

"Maybe he did."

***

With his lantern offering a little light inside the tent, the young lieutenant scratched out his thoughts into a journal.

"Have arrived at the scene of the massacre I was ordered to investigate. My scout believes the evidence at the scene suggests white perpetrators and not Indian as at first believed. This calls into question whether I should now turn the matter over to a law official, either the town marshal in Del Norte or the U.S. Marshal in Denver. The first is likely to be ill-equipped to investigate, and a deputy of the latter would take weeks to arrive, if he ever did. As the only official in the area, I am inclined to accept responsibility for the scene and endeavor to make an arrest of those responsible. My orders at the outset were to make a brief excursion in search of the Utes responsible. I am inclined to interpret my orders to extend to a search for whatever party is responsible for this massacre."

Turner blew the ink dry and shut the journal and then turned down the wick to envelop himself in darkness.

In reality, Turner's orders were to make the briefest of excursions – a show for the men wintering in Del Norte with an expectation of returning empty-handed. But if Stout was correct, and he seemed to be confident, the killings were not Indian hostilities but calculated murders by white men. But to what purpose? Were they intended to raise tension between the prospectors and the Indians? Was this some sort of act of revenge? Stout's cryptic answer that perhaps they did steal gold was not borne out by the evidence. The ore in the mules' packs would likely come to a healthy sum once the gold was stamped out of the quartz. If theft was the intention, the men had left quite a bit of money behind.

Turner's final thoughts of the day turned, as they often did, to his father. As he pulled his blanket up over himself, he wondered how many times his own father lay under a canvas tent pondering the day's events and wondering what tomorrow would bring. He'd been killed in combat at a place called Chancellorsville in Virginia. Turner had been about eight years old when he last saw his father as the man left for war, and Turner did not have much memory of the man prior to the war. He'd been raised by his uncle, who also fought in the war but returned home to a hero's welcome. Though his father had been a victim of battle, he had died bravely, and Turner's uncle had distinguished himself in the war. Turner's appointment to West Point was secured through the family's reputation.

And now the young lieutenant was desperate to cover himself in glory to not only justify his uncle's faith in him, but in a real way to live up to his family's name.

The young lieutenant had a phrase that seemed to always be repeating somewhere in the back of his mind: "Do them honor."

As he drifted to sleep, alone in the small tent, that thought repeated now. Whatever decision he made come sunrise, he must do honor to his father and his uncle.

His orders on paper were plain enough, investigate and pursue. But the verbal orders were murkier. Investigate and make a show of pursuing.

Sergeant O'Keefe had not been present when the colonel issued the orders. Only Levi Stout. No one in the expedition, other than the scout, knew that this mission was intended by the colonel to be largely ceremonial. Would Stout object to an aggressive pursuit?

If he stretched his orders to the limit and pursued the men responsible, he must find them quickly and nearby. Otherwise, he would be in defiance of his orders. And in that case, should his pursuit take him deep into the mountains, he must return with ultimate success, otherwise he would surely endure a loss of favor among his superior officers.

What West Point did not teach was how to walk a fine line.

- 3 -

Levi Stout watched his breath collect in a cloud in front of his face as he bent far forward to adjust his center of gravity and finish the climb these last few feet to the precipice of the ridge overlooking the trail.

"Helluva hike, it is," Sergeant O'Keefe said, his breath coming hard against the strenuous climb.

Lieutenant Turner, breathing just as hard but making no comment about it, straightened himself up and stopped for a moment. They were just a few yards shy of the ridge. The lieutenant turned and looked at slope they'd climbed. The hill presented an excellent view of the trail below and the river winding down into the valley. Men staging an ambush here would have seen their victims coming, and they'd have also seen if anyone else was approaching on the trail. And there were plenty of boulders and big cedar trees to give cover to the men in ambush.

Stout reached the top of the slope first, and he turned around and offered a hand back to Sergeant O'Keefe, pulling the man to the top. O'Keefe then helped the lieutenant.

The view was as breathtaking as the cold that seemed to snatch the air from the young lieutenant's chest.

To their south, the mountain peaks seemed to crest like waves on the sea caught in a moment of time. Ahead of them, to the west and north, the big, rocky cliffs rose like giant walls of the narrow canyon through which the river, over time unimaginable, had cut its path.

Turner stood for some time, catching his breath from the climb up the slope and admiring the view. There were views of mountains back east, of course, but none such as these.

"It is glorious," Turner said.

"This way, Lieutenant Turner," Stout said, starting along the ridge line.

The three men walked some distance and found themselves behind a cluster of firs.

"I reasoned they'd have to hide their horses somewhere," Stout said. "If you're down below, on the trail, you'd never see the horses on this ridge behind these trees. I found a trail – it's a longer walk, but easy for horses to make – that comes around from the north there and leads right up to here. I followed the trail and this is where I came yesterday looking for tracks."

Stout found the place where he'd swept away the snow. Only a little had fallen in its place, and he now brushed that away with his gloved hand. He had to be careful and use a light touch to avoid disturbing the track. One, in particular, was as clear as it could be.

"See this? How the track is sharp and narrow. You know what that means?"

"I do not," Turner admitted. O'Keefe stood aside, watching the two men kneeling in front of him, but not participating. It didn't do for a sergeant to show ignorance, and O'Keefe had no knowledge of reading tracks.

"That there track, Lieutenant Turner, was left by a shod horse. You could almost lay a horseshoe down inside that track it's so perfect. If that was a shoeless horse, you'd be able to see the cleft and the frog from the horse's foot."

Turner glanced at Stout and then looked to O'Keefe for an explanation.

"Injuns ride ponies with no shoes on their feet, Lieutenant," O'Keefe explained.

"Of course," Turner said, frustrated that he did not know a thing that was obvious and should have been known.

"It's possible they rode stolen horses," Stout said. "They might have raided a ranch down in the valley, taken some horses, and that would explain why they were riding horses with shoes. But I've had a look around here. You can see for yourself all the tracks. I figure there was nothing less than two dozen horses hid up on this ridge when they made the ambush, and as far as I can tell, every horse on this ridge was shod."

Lieutenant Turner made a show of examining some of the tracks, brushing away the snow the way Stout did it.

He could look at a track and determine the difference between a shod horse and one that was barefoot. At home, at his father's farm, hadn't he seen the prints left in the dirt outside the stables thousands of times, ever since he was a child? But it was different, reading a track and understanding its import. He might have seen those prints in the dirt at home, but he couldn't have said which one was the fresher, and he couldn't determine one horse from another by the tracks they left hours or days earlier. But Stout seemed to be able to see a book's worth of information in the tracks as he looked at them.

O'Keefe appeared to be disinterested, and Turner wondered if that was not also the role that he should play. Allow the scout to do his job, and O'Keefe to do his job, and Turner would do his. But the young lieutenant was eager to learn, to understand. Since coming west to Fort Garland, Turner had begun to suspect there was much out here to be learned that was not taught at West Point. And he wanted to understand. He was desperate to learn the ways of men like Levi Stout who seemed to have an intuitive knowledge of all the natural environment could show him.

Turner scanned the horizon from the ridge. He saw his surroundings the way he would have imagined them from a lecture in a classroom: Defensible positions, routes of attack, supply lines, avenues of retreat. His was a grand view, a perception on the scale of armies. The young lieutenant found himself envious of the scout who could peer into the small details and read a story.

"So we are more confirmed in our suspicion that these were not Indians who attacked this party of prospectors?" Lieutenant Turner said. "Can you follow their trail?"

"Not easily," Stout said. "Not with snow covering the ground that wasn't here when they set out. The best I could do is surmise which way they've gone and then try to confirm it as we follow along."

"How would you confirm it?" Turner asked.

"Sign. Droppings from the horses. Campsites. It's a large party of men who ambushed these prospectors. They would not be able to hide their trail easily."

O'Keefe snorted derisively, and Turner raised his eyebrows at him.

"Sergeant?"

"All's I'm saying, Lieutenant Turner, is them men who done this isn't likely to stay up in the mountains," the Irishman said. "Ten days it's been since they made this attack. We've little reason to believe they'd yet be around."

"Mr. Stout?" Turner said, looking to the scout to make some objection.

"They done this ambush and slaughter for a reason," Stout said. "Two dozen men, or whatever their number, they don't commit murders like this for sport. And there's only one reason I can think of."

"And what is that?" Turner asked.

"They're looking to steal a claim. My guess is they committed this ambush on these prospectors and then went to the claim. Whether they're still there, whether we can catch them, I don't know."

"Do we know where the claim might be?" Turner asked.

"No, sir. But if we follow their trail, assuming I can find it, we might be able to catch them at the place."

"Best to turn the matter over to the U.S. Marshal in Denver," O'Keefe said. "Claim jumping isn't an army concern."

"As the ranking officer here, I'll make the determination what's an army concern and what's not," Turner said sharply. "Surmise which way they've gone, Mr. Stout."

- 4 -

Jacob Stallings despised the cold. He sat by the fire, huddled in a heavy bearskin coat that had been a gift from his brother, a coat made from a bear that Lou himself had brought down. The other men seemed to get along fine in the snow, the wind, the cold. But Jacob despised it. It was getting late in the day, but all through the afternoon it never did warm up any. The wind bit mighty cold, especially here among the tall cedars where the sun's rays were so interrupted by the canopy.

Nevertheless, he was a precise man, and his thoroughness in his job did not allow him to do a job halfway. So he had endured the cold, and he would come out of this misery a wealthy man.

"You have all you need?" Lou asked him, coming over to the fire.

"I do," Jacob said. "We can give exact plats to the land office to secure a patent on the claim. We have samples enough to prove the value of the claim."

Lou Stallings slid his gloves from his hands and held his hands out to the fire. The gloves offered little protection against the cold, and his fingers stung.

"A lot of griping among the men," Lou said. "We should start out in the morning. We'll be five days getting down to Del Norte."

"We'll go in the morning," Jacob said.

Lou picked up a leather-bound satchel of papers.

"What's this?" he asked.

Jacob reached out and took it back from him.

"Kindling," Jacob Stallings said darkly. "Those are the claim papers I took off the prospectors. They had it all prepared."

Lou chuckled.

"Just scratch out their names and write in Stallings Brothers & Company," Lou said.

"That's basically what I've done here," he said, nodding to a similar leather-bound satchel that had his own plats and claim filing on the same claim.

This was not the first time the two brothers had run a theft of a mine, though this was by far the biggest.

For eight years, the Stallings brothers had worked the eastern range. They'd filed a number of claims on promising strikes and sold those claims to companies with the capital to hire the men and bring in the equipment necessary to sink shafts and work the claims. They'd sell this claim, too, but this one was special. Based on the success of previous claims, the Stallings brothers had worked for the past two years for one company, getting paid a monthly salary to find a big strike. Their agreement, in addition to the salary, included a one-third ownership of any profitable mine. All they had to do was find the right lode and they'd never have to swing another pick or climb another cliff or spend another night in a tent. The company they were working for would bear the costs of getting at the ore and the Stallings brothers would own a third of it.

With this incentive, the Stallings brothers had sought a guarantee.

Earlier in the season, they'd heard about a big strike a group of men were working in the San Juan Mountains west of Del Norte, and they came to see it for themselves. Posing as regular prospectors, they went to the diggings and saw that the men had indeed found a vein of high-grade gold, and everything suggested that the vein went deep into the mountain.

"It might be a million dollars' worth of gold down in that mountain," Jacob Stallings told his brother. Jacob Stallings was a trained mineralogist, and Lou trusted his younger brother's education. Jacob had done right by the two of them in the past, and they'd earned a decent living selling mines that turned profitable. But this was their chance to do what every prospector in the hills hoped to do – strike it rich. Neither of the Stallings boys had any qualms that they'd had to kill the prospectors who actually found this claim. Rare was the man in these mountains who could afford to keep a conscience.

In the days since the massacre, the Stallings brothers

and their men had made some improvements to the claim. They'd dug a little deeper and obtained new samples. They'd felled some trees to erect an open shelter – it wasn't the sort of thing that would get them through the winter, but they could get their tents under the solid shelter. More importantly, they could affix stamped metal signs with the name "Stallings Brothers & Company" to the more permanent shelter, and it would give their claim an air of legitimacy.

Jacob Stallings had spent enough time panning the small stream below the find and shoveling dirt around it. He had confidence this claim would set him and his brother up for life. A house in California, away from these crippling winters, away from these rough towns and rough men.

From down below, the two Stallings brothers could hear riders approaching. Lou Stallings stood up and picked up his rifle, craning his neck to get a look through the trees at the trail.

"It's Tommy Iron and Phil Wells," Lou said, setting the rifle back down. He watched, though, as the two riders made their way up the switchback trail that led higher to where the diggings were located. The men seemed to ride with an urgency, and something about the way they sat in their saddles suggested to Lou that they had bad news.

Tommy and Phil were among the most trusted of the men Lou had hired for this expedition. They were, like the others, hard men who didn't mind doing a hard job. Veterans, mostly, who didn't balk at killing, and all men who'd served hard time in sentences of bad luck. If he'd said it once, Lou had said to Jacob a thousand times, "Give me a veteran who's down and out, and I'll show you a man who will do any job you put in front of him."

Whether it was digging or building or killing, Lou always tried to hire hard-luck veterans.

"What's the matter?" Lou asked as the two riders came up to the pavilion and dismounted.

"Soldiers down below," Tommy Irons said. "They've been to the trail where we killed those men, and they're coming this way."

Lou frowned and glanced back at Jacob.

"That's bad news," Jacob Stallings said, and he gave his older brother a deliberate glare. "You said we'd have fifteen days."

"I didn't think news would reach the fort so fast," Lou said with a shrug. He turned back to Tommy Irons. "How many, Tommy?"

"Ten troopers," Tommy said. "They've got a young lieutenant in charge. But there's also a scout with them, and he's the one tracking us."

"Tracking us?" Lou said. "How the hell?"

Tommy Irons shrugged.

"He's a good scout. He's coming on intuition more than anything else, but his intuition is solid."

"How do you know he's a good scout?" Lou asked.

Tommy Irons was the only one among the group who wasn't a veteran from the War Between the States. Tommy Irons was a half-breed Pawnee who scouted for the cavalry in the Indian Wars. He sometimes still did, though Lou did not doubt Tommy's loyalty to the outfit. Lou had paid them all a little up front, but they knew the big payoff came when Jacob Stallings sold this claim. Every man in the outfit stood to make two hundred dollars, and that was enough money to buy loyalty. Tommy Irons would take a long time earning two hundred dollars scouting for the army.

"It's Levi Stout. I know him."

"How good is he?" Lou asked.

"Good enough that with our trail being almost two weeks old and hid under fresh snowfall, he's still tracking us."

"We're leaving out in the morning," Jacob Stallings interjected. "Can we avoid them?"

"Unless they take a different trail and wander off in the wrong direction, we'll meet them coming up as we're going down," Tommy Irons said. "And I don't think Levi Stout will take a wrong trail."

Lou and Jacob exchanged a look.

"How many men are they?" Lou asked.

"Eight troopers. A sergeant and the lieutenant, and the scout."

"Eleven, altogether, then," Lou said. "Maybe the Utes who attacked that party of prospectors should also attack the cavalrymen."

Tommy Irons shrugged indifferently.

"If you do that, you best make sure not to leave any sign that it was white men and not Utes," Tommy said. "You slaughter a cavalry patrol, and you guarantee the army will come looking for whoever done it."

Lou took his seat by his brother.

"These ain't prospectors," he said. "These are fighting men. Be best to try to catch them early, maybe before they get moving. Surround their camp, rush them, catch them off guard."

Jacob Stallings nodded.

"Take enough men to get it done," Jacob said. "I'll stay back with whoever is left and we'll break camp at dawn and meet you on the trail on the way out. You take care of the soldiers, and in five days we'll have the claim filed and then we'll head to Denver. In two months, we'll be rich."

DAY ONE

- 5 -

The soldiers woke before dawn.

Sergeant O'Keefe had the men build two campfires, and he positioned himself between the two fires while the troopers prepared breakfast. Coffee and bacon and biscuits.

Lieutenant Turner stood a ways away from the men with Levi Stout. The scout frustrated the lieutenant. He remained vague about what he knew and what he guessed of the tracks of the men. Turner could not determine, from what Stout had told him, if they had any reasonable expectation that they were on the right trail.

"My gut tells me that these men have come this way," Stout said. "They left the ore samples with the men they killed, and if it's claim jumping, then they would go back to the dig to get their own samples so that they can file a patent for a claim."

"But how do you know that this is the way to the claim?" Turner asked.

The cavalry patrol made its camp in clearing in the middle of a forest of spruce and pine. The trail they followed was little more than a deer path, but here – under the canopy of the trees – little snow had reached the ground. Levi Stout took the lieutenant by the elbow and led him several yards away from the camp.

"Do you see these tracks here?" Stout asked.

Turner kneeled low to get a better look. Beneath the thin bed of pine straw, on the dirt path, Turner saw what he recognized as a deer print. It was a good-sized deer, one that any hunter would gladly track.

"Deer," Turner said.

"That one, yes," Stout agreed. "That's a fresh track. That deer was here yesterday afternoon. You can tell because of the way it's sunk in. That track was made in mud, since the snowfall. But I'm talking about these here that are just traces on the surface."

Stout gently brushed away some pine straw so that Turner could see the light prints on the ground. Then he traced with his finger what he wanted the lieutenant to see.

"This one here, this is definitely mule," Stout said. "Smaller, more oblong, and the frog is larger. See that 'V' there, how wide it is? Mule. And it's headed east, headed out. I figure this track was made ten days, maybe two weeks ago. The mule that left this track is dead now, over that massacre. I'd wager a month's pay on it. But this one here, that's a horse print. If nothing else, you can see the shoe and know it was a horse that stepped here. It's over a mule track, see that? So the horse came through here since the mule did, though both of them came through within a few days of each other. And the horse, he's headed back into the mountains."

Lieutenant Turner stood up.

"Is that proof?" he asked.

"Not proof, as such," Stout said. "Any mule and any horse could have put those tracks there. But as I look around, I see plenty of horse tracks – it was a large party mounted on horses. Some of this is just me guessing, but my guess is that these are the tracks of the party that did that massacre. But I cannot say that I followed the tracks here and know for certain what party left them."

"How much farther in are they going to be?" Turner asked with a glance to the cloudy morning sky. "Those clouds threaten snow. I do not want to be caught in bad snow storm."

"They could be five miles or a hundred," Stout said. "And I can't predict the weather. It's your choice, Lieutenant Turner, if we go on or turn back."

"What's your gut tell you, Mr. Stout, about how much farther along those men might be?"

Stout sighed heavily through his nose, the air audible as it passed through his thick mustache, and he twisted his lips so that his thick beard turned one way and then the other. Without comment, Stout began to walk along the deer path, traipsing over the tracks he'd just shown to the lieutenant. Turner took a delicate step, placing a toe on a patch of pine straw where he thought he would not disturb the tracks. But Stout kept going, not heeding the tracks at all.

"Is it okay to walk on the tracks?" Turner asked.

Stout stopped and turned around to look at the lieutenant.

"Nothing more those tracks can tell us, one way or another. Don't hurt nothing to walk across 'em now."

Turner nodded, and he followed the scout along the path. They walked some distance so that they came out of sight of the camp, though they had not yet escaped the rich smell of the cedar wood burning in the campfires. As they moved along the trail, Turner noted the way the trail seemed to drop down a steep slope, and shortly they emerged from the evergreen forest with a view of a wide, grassy valley – the grass still largely covered in snow. Down below a wide but shallow creek meandered through the valley. They also now had a view of the peaks and rocky cliffs of the mountains around them.

Levi Stout pointed off to the southwest.

"I would put them somewhere on that mountain, the one where you can see the peak right there," he said. "Maybe five to ten miles. It's a guess, but that's where I reckon the claim must be."

"What makes you think so?" Turner asked, hoping for some insight into the scout's intuition.

Stout grunted. He did not like explaining himself, and the lieutenant seemed full of questions for everything Stout said to him.

"If it's claim jumping, like I think it must be, then the claim has to be in a remote spot. Judging from what I can see, not many people have come through here these past few months. Prospectors leave a lot of sign, more than the snow would cover. They leave fire rings. They leave empty cans and other bits of trash. They cut down saplings and knock down branches and widen trails. No, sir, this valley here, and the river, didn't attract the prospectors in heavy numbers this past season. Maybe next year, especially if this jumped claim proves out. But if you want to jump a claim without folks knowing that's what you're doing, you have to find a paying claim that doesn't have a lot of other people around it."

Lieutenant Turner nodded as he followed along with the logic.

Prospecting for gold, digging, making a claim – these were all things foreign to him. But it seemed clear that Stout knew his business.

"Then we should go to that mountain," Turner said. "Five to ten miles? We can be there in a few hours. We'll have a look. If we find nothing, we'll start back this afternoon for Fort Garland."

Stout nodded.

"If that suits you, that suits me."

Lieutenant Turner started to say something else, but Levi Stout shushed him. The scout's brow furrowed as he strained his ears to hear something, but Lieutenant Turner did not know what.

"Did you hear something?" Turner whispered.

"It's not what I hear," Stout whispered back, speaking softly through his heavy whiskers. "No, it's what I don't hear. The birds have stopped chirping."

"What does that mean?" Turner asked.

The answer came as horrendous squall, a guttural shout. And then it was taken up by others, so that the squall became a prolonged pandemonium, seemingly dozens of voices raised up in a burst of violence. There were shouts mixed in with the ballyhoo, and Turner felt a sick feeling in his gut as his blood seemed to turn cold. He started to run back toward the forest and the trail they'd taken, but the scout grabbed him by the arm and held him back.

"We'll go, but we won't run in there," Levi Stout said. "That's a sure way to get ourselves killed. You follow me, Lieutenant."

He did not give voice to it, but in his mind, Levi Stout cursed himself for a fool for leaving his gun back at camp.

***

Levi Stout made his way swiftly back into the woods, going at a jog but now avoiding the path they'd followed out. Instead, he cut through the brush and fallen trees, under branches and through the springy foliage of the firs. Lieutenant Turner followed behind him, unsnapping the flap on his holster and drawing out his revolver. He did not have percussion caps on any of the cylinders, though there was a ball in each cylinder. Nevertheless, the lieutenant felt better for having the gun in his hand.

Ahead of them, still, they could hear shouts and other sounds of struggle, but whatever was occurring back at the camp seemed to be coming to an end. The noise receded as the scout and lieutenant dashed toward it.

Now, after jogging some distance through the woods, Levi Stout came to a sudden, skidding stop, and he dropped down to the earth under the cover of a thick mass of cedar branches.

Lieutenant Turner followed him to the ground, and there he opened the pouch on his belt containing caps for the gun. He bit the finger of his glove and slid a hand out of the glove so that he could finger the caps. One by one, Turner armed the cylinders of his revolver.

Stout pushed forward so that he could see the campsite through the branches of the fir, and what he saw made him draw back.

A party of mostly white men had fallen upon the troopers of the cavalry patrol, and they must have done it with terrific speed and stealth. The shouts must have come at the final moment as the party rushed the troopers, for the cavalrymen had been completely overwhelmed. Even now, most of the men in blue uniforms were slumped over logs or sprawled on the ground. One man's body lay atop one of the smoldering campfires.

Across the campsite, though, three cavalrymen had gathered and made a stand and were still fighting. They'd drawn their swords, and as Stout watched, one of them swung his sword and opened a vicious gash across the chest of one the attackers. The men stood no chance, though. Stout could see that all three of the cavalrymen had already suffered wounds – each man had blood smearing his face, and one had an injury to his forehead visible even from this distance.

Worse, the injured men had drawn the attention of nearly all the assailants inside the camp. Stout figured it must be fifteen or twenty men making the attack, though there was still too much confusion to properly count them. Those three men, making this final stand, would be overwhelmed in moments.

But one other had drawn the attention of a couple of the attackers, and he now had Stout's attention, too.

Sergeant O'Keefe, wounded was crawling along the ground. The sergeant appeared to have a severe wound on his leg. He was making for the trees not far from where Stout and Lieutenant Turner huddled in their hidden position. Two men among the party who had ambushed the cavalry were now walking toward O'Keefe. Both men were armed with fighting knives and clubs. They did not hurry – the sergeant's progress was slow as he tried to flee with a badly wounded leg.

"We must help him," Turner whispered through gritted teeth.

"Hush, unless you want to die right here," Stout bit back. "Don't shoot that gun, and don't move from these trees."

For a moment, Turner thought the scout was exhibiting cowardice. But then Stout positioned himself on all fours, cat-like, and Turner realized that Stout intended to pounce.

And then it came in a blur.

As the two armed men approached O'Keefe, were nearly on top of him, Levi Stout sprang from the cover of the trees. He rushed at the men, his big knife clutched in his hand, and fell upon them with such ferocity that the two men were immediately rendered useless.

Stout ran right past the first man, but he swung his blade at that man as he passed.

From his position under the trees, the lieutenant believed that Stout had missed the man.

Stout then leapt on the second man, and the two of

them went to the ground in a heap. By closing the distance and jumping on the man, he'd immobilized him, preventing the man from countering with his weapons. Stout's heavy frame came to rest on the other man, and then the army scout rose up, the knife high in the air, and he plunged it back down into the man's breast. He repeated the movement three or four more times.

Turner prepared to go after the first one, the man Stout had run past, but now the lieutenant realized that he'd not missed the man at all. Instead, Stout's blade had thoroughly sliced the other man's throat. The man stood now, clenching his hands at his neck as if to hold the wound closed. Stout now turned back to this first man and plunged the knife into the man's back. They both went down to the ground now, and Turner watched as Stout wrenched the knife free and then buried the knife into the man's back a second time.

Brutal.

Lieutenant Turner's stomach turned.

He knew that combat brought horror. He knew veterans, men who served with his uncle, who now showed no obvious sign of injury yet daily took morphine, and he'd heard his uncle say many times that these men took morphine to ease the pain of the scars of the mind. Turner believed his uncle spoke from a place of understanding, and it frightened him to think that men saw things, even committed acts, that haunted them so thoroughly in their minds that without a limp or a missing limb or a shattered face they might still seek to medicate themselves with copious doses of morphine.

But now, in a moment, Lieutenant Turner's entire perspective shifted.

Brutal murder, done by hand, so close that Stout

could hear the man's death rattle.

A cold chill swept through the young lieutenant. So eager he'd been to prove himself and drape himself in glory. But seeing glory so close had rattled Turner. He found himself paralyzed – not with fear, but from shock. This was not what he expected.

Stout rolled away from the man he'd just killed and got up beside Sergeant O'Keefe. He stayed low to the ground. Turner watched him. Stout checked over his shoulder to be sure he wasn't seen, and then he scooped up the sergeant in his arms and man-handled him into the dense cedar branches beside Turner.

Stout was breathing heavy, and O'Keefe was grunting from the pain of his opened leg.

"You'll have to quiet that, Sergeant, or we're all dead," Stout said.

The scout raised up on his knees and his fingers reached down to his belt. His fingers moved deftly, and in a moment, he had the leather scabbard for his knife off the belt. He slid the knife from it and put the leather in O'Keefe's mouth.

"If it hurts, bite against that, Sergeant," Stout said. "But quit your moaning. If they hear you, we're all three dead."

Now, with two quick swings of his arm, Stout brought down cedar boughs from the back side of the tree, and he shoved those forward to provide more cover between them and the men doing slaughter in the campsite. Then, Stout dropped to his stomach to lay under the cedar branches with the lieutenant and O'Keefe.

"If you're religious, you should pray that we ain't seen, Lieutenant Turner. We can't fight them men, and we won't outrun 'em, neither."

Beyond the evergreen boughs, the ghastly business of slaughter continued.

So far as Lieutenant Turner could see, all the men of his patrol were now murdered. But their assailants had not quit. Now several of them had gone to work cutting the hair from the corpses of the cavalrymen.

"That's why they didn't use guns," Stout whispered. "They've attacked with spears and clubs to continue their ruse that it's the Utes. And they're scalping them now for that same purpose."

While some of the men scalped, a couple of them began to untie the mounts from the lines they'd been tied to overnight. They waved their hats and slapped the horses on the rumps to chase them off.

"Damn," Stout said. "Lost our horses now, too."

O'Keefe gave a groan even though he bit hard on Stout's leather scabbard, and Stout looked at the man. He seemed barely conscious, his eyes rolling. The wound on his leg was deep and severe, but beyond that he had a large welt on his forehead where he'd been knocked with a club.

"We've got to get him out of here or he's sure to give us away," Stout said. "Help me, Lieutenant."

Turner nodded, and together the two men lifted O'Keefe and began making their way through the forest, away from the scene of slaughter. Even toting the weight of the injured sergeant, Stout moved quickly, though Turner did not feel that they were fleeing. Stout's movement was deliberate, not panicked or hurried. But he also did not exhibit a moment of indecision. He picked his route and kept moving.

"What about my men?" Turner said, stalling the escape. "That was murder – awful, bloody murder."

"Don't think about that now, Lieutenant. There's time enough to think on that later."

- 6 -

Lou Stallings stood near the two fallen men and surveyed the scene around them.

"Nobody saw what happened to them?" he asked generally to those around. Most of the men were here now. Tommy Irons had discovered the two dead men. Other than a few scrapes and bloodied noses, these were the only casualties from Stallings' party. And they were both dead with many stab wounds. None of the men spoke up. If anyone had seen anything, he wasn't going to say so now. That would be admitting that he'd seen two of their men get killed and hadn't intervened.

"Three from the cavalry are missing," Tommy Irons

said. "Including the scout, there were eleven of them. We've only got eight bodies here. Levi Stout got away, along with two others."

Lou sniffed and looked around. This was a layer of trouble he'd not planned for.

"We can't have survivors," Lou said. "Everything hinges on these massacres being put down to the Injuns. If a trooper walks out of here and says what really happens, not only are we not getting paid, but we'll all be swinging from a rope."

Tommy Irons saw the cut boughs under the cedar tree and went to investigate.

"They hid here," he reported in a moment. "At least one of them is hurt. There's blood on the ground here, and a fair amount."

"Can you track them?" Lou Stallings asked, walking to where Tommy Irons knelt near the base of the cedars, pushing branches out of his face.

Tommy Irons grunted.

"I can track them, I reckon," he said. "Be no harder than tracking a shot elk. One of them is bleeding bad."

There was too much to do. Lou needed to meet back up with Jacob and the small party still at the diggings who were supposed to be breaking camp. They were going to leave out of the mountains today. He needed to finish here at this scene, make certain there was no evidence of who perpetrated the massacre on the soldiers. That meant burying his two killed me, too, and burying them someplace far away where they wouldn't be found. And now, added to his other troubles, he had three cavalrymen who escaped the ambush.

"We've got to find them," Lou said.

He had eighteen men with him. Well, sixteen now. They should have been more than enough to overwhelm the troopers, and Lou wasn't sure how three of them managed to escape.

It was good that Jacob was not here. Jacob ran the outfit. Lou was the muscle, and most of the men looked to Lou, but Jacob made all the plans. The trouble with Jacob was that he was indecisive. He took a long time to weigh all the factors before creating a plan. Jacob was thorough and precise, and his plans typically fell into place. But he wouldn't be good right now. He'd spend too long coming to a conclusion. Now they needed Lou's decisiveness, and Lou reached a decision in a hurry.

"Wells, you take three men and bury these two," he said. "You go off someplace deep in the woods, or you find a gulch where no one is going to wander, and you get rid of these bodies in a way that means nobody finds them. Strip them, too. Make sure they don't have any letters or papers of any kind, no tags in their clothes. If a wolf digs them up, I don't want anyone to be able to identify them because of something in their pockets. So strip them bare. When you've done that, you go up and meet with Jacob. Tell him what's happened. I'm taking the rest of the men and going after these three troopers. They won't get far. We'll meet up with you and Jacob on your way out to Del Norte."

Phil Wells, who'd fought beside Lou Stallings in the war, was about the only man in this outfit that Lou trusted as much as he trusted his own brother. Phil was a sturdy man. He didn't balk at hard duty, and he never questioned an order. He was the sort who was competent and could be left alone and counted on to do a job.

Now Lou turned to Tommy Irons.

"Let's get together the others and go find these three."

- 7 -

"We need to get back to our supplies," Levi Stout said. "O'Keefe doesn't survive this if we can't treat his leg proper. And you and I need rifles."

Even as he spoke, Levi Stout used his knife to cut O'Keefe's suspenders and he wrapped the injured leg to hold the wound closed. The gash ran almost the length of his thigh. He'd been cut by a hatchet. The wound was deep, and it bled, but it looked to Stout like the artery was not cut – he wasn't bleeding so much that death was imminent.

Lieutenant Turner did not know what to do, and he did not like it.

Nothing at West Point had prepared him for the decimation of his command and to find himself virtually alone and fleeing from an overwhelming force. This was the reality that the text books did not cover.

"First thing is getting this leg bandaged," Stout said. "Second thing is getting our weapons. Third thing is getting back to Del Norte and then on to the fort."

"We should wait them out," Turner said.

Stout grunted in disagreement.

"They're going to come after us," Stout said. "These men have gone to lengths to make it look like the Utes are on the warpath, and they're not likely to let us live to say otherwise."

O'Keefe had recovered some from the knock to the head, and his earlier groaning was now replaced by heavy breathing and a constant stream of oaths against the pain muttered under his breath.

"Lieutenant, you and Mr. Stout leave me and get back to Del Norte. Send word to the fort for more men and come back for me," O'Keefe said. He did not offer it as a heroic gesture. The man wanted revenge, and he wanted to see that party of men who'd killed his troopers hanging from ropes.

"We'll not leave you, Sergeant," Turner said. "We're all of us getting back to Del Norte and to Fort Garland."

With Levi Stout carrying Sergeant O'Keefe on his back, the three of them had made their way through the cedar and ponderosa pines. They emerged from the forest on the slope of a narrow gulch. Ahead and below, they found the slopes on either side of the gulch were grassy and open. Higher on the slope ahead of them, rocky sandstone cliffs jutted toward the sky, and into the face of those cliffs the water and wind of centuries had carved structures that enough resembled battlements that the lieutenant immediately pointed up to the cliffs and said, "There!"

Levi Stout made the climb up the steep slope with the sergeant on his back and the lieutenant trying to steady the injured man. When at last they found a crevice wide enough for the three of them, Stout bent low and leaned to roll the sergeant off his back. O'Keefe roughly hit the rocky ground, but he was coming back to consciousness now, and being sprawled on the rocky soil was significantly better than being constantly jostled on the scout's back.

The sun had melted most of the snow from the exposed slopes of the gulch, but Stout felt certain he and the lieutenant had left any number of tracks in what snow there was. He distinctly remembered hearing the crunch of icy snow under his feet as he made his way up the slope to their hiding place. So while they were hidden from view of any cursory glance, if those men who attacked the troopers pursued – and Stout was positively certain they would – a more thorough survey of the ground would undoubtedly lead the men directly to the scout and the two cavalrymen.

"We cannot hide here long, Lieutenant," Stout warned. "They'll find us sure, here."

Turner balled a fist and punched his hand in frustration. His first sole command – a simple task, really nothing more than leading a burial party when broken down to its essence, and just to put on a show for the prospectors to give them a sense that the army had not abandoned them – and somehow, he had utterly and completely failed and all of his troopers were now dead. Disgrace and dishonor, likely a court martial. And the worst of it was, he now had absolutely no idea how to

move forward. Had it not been for the presence of the wounded sergeant and the gritty scout, Turner thought he might have wept with despair.

"Lieutenant?" Stout prompted.

"I'm open to suggestions, Mr. Stout," Turner admitted.

This was the answer the scout had hoped for. Unlike the lieutenant, whose knowledge came from lectures in a classroom, the scout had practical experience, and he'd already devised a plan. Granted, his plan relied heavily on his own abilities – something the lieutenant would not have conceived.

"Sergeant O'Keefe's condition is a problem for us," Stout said. "We can't move fast with the sergeant's gashed leg. But we can't make a stand, neither. We don't have arms to do it. We need horses and we need guns. We need to be able to treat Sergeant O'Keefe's injury, and we need provisions enough to see us out of these mountains and back to Del Norte. The only way we get all that is by going back to the campsite. I can do it. I can get us guns and horses and supplies, but I can't do it – and avoid those men – with the two of you with me. So we need to find a place where you and Sergeant O'Keefe can hole up and not be found."

Turner looked at the tall cliffs reaching above them toward the morning sky. The clouds that had left everything gray and cold were gone, and the sun was rising into a bright, bluebird sky. The cliffs loomed, craggy and dangerous.

"We won't go up," Turner said.

But Levi Stout had already figured that, and he was crouched low at the edge of the outcropping where they hid, looking into the gulch below. A dozen aspens, their leaves fading from gold to brown, clustered at the bottom of the gulch. There, at the very base of it, was a small stream, and in places along that creek there was shrub brush. A deer might hide in there unseen, but not two hunted men.

Stout frowned in frustration, and now he scanned the cliffs. He pointed to a spot above the forest they'd come through where a crevice formed what almost looked like a natural trail seemed to lead to the looming precipice above.

"That might be the way," Stout said.

The snow had collected deep in the narrow V of that crevice, but as Stout surveyed it with his eyes, he thought they could probably make their way on the slopes and not step in the snow. It might be enough that their pursuers would not think they'd gone through that way and would leave them be. The important thing would be to move quickly and not leave a single track. Once he had the lieutenant and the sergeant at the top of the cliffs, he could come back down and leave tracks down into the gulch. Even if it meant jogging a mile or so down through the gulch, leaving tracks for their pursuers to follow, and then finding a way to double back, it seemed like the only feasible plan.

"Help me hoist Sergeant O'Keefe up on my back," Stout said. "Follow me, and don't step in snow – not anywhere. Not even the toe of your boot."

Stout picked his path carefully. Though the slopes of the gulch were nearly bare of snow, there was still plenty of it nestled in shady places between rocks and on the grass. If the sky remained cloudless the slopes of this canyon would surely be bare by tomorrow afternoon.

When they got to the crevice, Stout realized it was

steeper than he'd thought.

"You're going to have to hold tight, Sergeant," Stout said.

Bearing the man's weight slowed him down, and picking his footfalls so carefully made it all the more difficult, but Stout managed to make the climb about halfway up. But there the natural trail ended, and Stout found himself again faced with vertical cliffs.

"We can't go higher," he told the lieutenant. "You'll just have to do your best here. If they find you, use your position on the high ground to fight them off."

Turner nodded, accepting whatever fate came to him.

Stout was satisfied that he was leaving the young lieutenant in the best possible position. The ledge where the sergeant and lieutenant were now huddled was hidden from below by large boulders. Those men who attacked the troopers would have to decide to take a look up the crevice before they would see the lieutenant. The crevice was narrow. If the attackers did find them and came at them, they'd have to come one at a time. It was steep enough that a determined man could fend off several men.

"If you have to use your gun, make every shot count," Stout advised. "I'll do my best to lead them away from you, and I'll be back in a couple of hours, hopefully with guns and horses."

***

Levi Stout made his way down the gulch, but his mind was elsewhere. He thought of Faustina, the Mexican woman he'd taken up with. Her people became Americans when their San Luis valley home became part of the United States back in '48. She was born an American a year later, though for most of her life that meant nothing. She was raised speaking Spanish and still spoke it most of the time. She was the youngest of seven children, and her father had not liked it when she took up with an Anglo. But he'd grown to accept Levi Stout, even if he never truly liked his son-in-law.

Faustina did not like for him to go to the fort. It always meant he'd be away for days, sometimes weeks, and she wouldn't have any word of him until he turned back up. She never knew if he was chasing Indians through the San Luis Valley or running dispatches to Fort Union. She liked it better when he went with the freight wagons down to Santa Fe. It was ten days, usually, there and back. It was predictable work, and seldom dangerous.

She had the temper common among her people's women and was known to sometimes throw things about their cabin. But when her dander wasn't up, she was a kind-hearted woman, and Stout believed that she likely loved him. At least, she did seem to care for him. Stout earned a decent enough living that Faustina's life was improved by being with him, and they talked often of having children and maybe even taking up residence in Santa Fe where life was a little easier. It was a dream that he'd not dared to dream in his previous life. But now – now it did not seem so farfetched, the thought of a little hacienda in the valley with the mountains visible from the front door, some cattle, and maybe a little family with sons and maybe a daughter or two playing chase while his wife makes dinner.

As far as Faustina went, Levi Stout could not resist her brown eyes, her black hair, her tan skin. When he wrapped his big hands around her narrow waist, she made him feel like a wild animal. He'd never known before that it was possible for a man to feel so much for a woman.

Stout made his way down to the tree line. He went fast, but he was careful. He expected the attackers had already begun their pursuit, though it was possible it took time. Maybe they did not realize right away that three men had escaped. Maybe it took them some time to decide what to do about it. And maybe none of them were adept at tracking. It could be that it would take them hours to find a trail.

From the tree line, Stout deliberately made his steps. He took short steps and wide steps and unnecessary steps, all in an effort to make his tracks appear to be those of two or three men instead of one, and he deliberately stepped in patches of snow. Now he wanted these tracks to be seen. In this manner, he continued making his way down the slope – hurrying over those places where there was no snow and he did not have to take steps for two. Down in the bottom of the gulch, he found deeper snow and here he was delayed as he again had to make steps that appeared to be from two men. He stepped down and then stepped over the track hoping to cause some obfuscation so that a good tracker would not see that all the tracks came from one man.

It was tedious and time consuming, but Stout knew that what he did here might mean life or death for the lieutenant and Sergeant O'Keefe.

He crossed the stream and got up to the opposite slope where there was no snow, and he hurried along the slope until he came to another good patch of snow. Here he left deliberate tracks again. He twisted around at one point, looking behind him, and was satisfied. He'd left a clearly visible trail, and Stout was confident that if those men who attacked the troopers pursued, they would not give a second thought to the cliffs where the lieutenant and O'Keefe hunkered down and waited. They would come on, following the tracks that they could not miss. And he believed he'd done a good enough job that not even a skilled tracker would realize his ruse.

He continued to climb up the slope, making for the trees at the top of the rounded hill. There he would not have to worry about snow and not have to worry so much about leaving tracks that would confound pursuers. Under the trees there would be less snow, it would not be as obvious that only one man had come through. The trick now was to find the right place to double back and get in behind anyone who might be coming after him, and then to work his way back to the campsite.

Stout was certain he'd be able to get clear of anyone who might be in pursuit and make his was back to the camp, but after that he didn't have as much confidence in how it would go.

Luck would play a part in what happened next. The men who attacked the troopers, they would have to be clear of the campsite. If they left any men behind, either to watch for the survivors or to steal provisions and weapons, he'd have a helluva time trying to fight them if it was more than just one or two that he could take by surprise. Stout was armed only with his knife. When he and Lieutenant Turner had left the camp earlier, Stout left his saddle gun and his carbine. That had been foolish, but he never would have believed these men to be so bold as to attack a cavalry patrol. The claim they were jumping, Stout figured, must be a big one.

Luck would determine whether he could catch a horse. If he could get his hands on one, he could track and rope two more. He'd seen that party who attacked the troopers drive off the horses. There was a good chance the horses wouldn't go far, but maybe the men rounded them up – stole them or killed them.

The sun wasn't yet halfway across the sky, and already it had been a disaster of a day. What Levi Stout needed now was a little bit of luck.

The scout trekked half a mile or more through the woods when saw that the tree line dropped down into the gulch and the trees were close on either side of the little stream. He realized, too, that the gulch ahead was narrowing and if he continued on, he would have to climb higher. The stream actually flowed from up above and dropped down into the gulch in a narrow waterfall, and it formed a pool before flowing down the way he'd already come. If he was going to double back, the place to do it would be down where the trees ran all the way up to the narrow stream, before he reached the pool below the waterfall.

So Stout now started to make his way lower. The slope here was steep and the trees more sparse so that there was less cover to hide in should anyone come looking. But he had to make his way carefully. He could not leave tracks in mud or snow here. He had to make his way going from one rock to the next, sometimes standing on his tiptoes to avoid stepping in mud.

He made a careful survey of the hillsides on either side of the gulch to be sure there was no one there watching, and then he hurried across the stream. It was wide enough here that he could not jump it, but it was just a shallow stream and would not come above his boots. Still, as he stepped down into the stream, Stout immediately felt the frigid water swirl around his boots. His toes were suddenly like ice, even though he had thick wool socks.

He didn't worry about making tracks in the stream – the bed was carpeted in pebbles big and small. But coming up the opposite bank was tedious work.

And then he was clear of the mud, back in among the trees. He did not think he was seen. He'd heard nothing from any pursuers. He'd seen nothing. If anyone was behind him, it had to be a small party, and Stout did not think these were the sort of men who would come after him with a small group.

- 8 -

Elliot Turner put a hand on his sergeant's shoulder. He meant for it to be a reassuring, calming hand, but the young lieutenant did not feel particularly reassured nor calm.

The slaughter of his command had been horrible to witness, both as the lieutenant who those men looked to for leadership and as a human being witnessing the gruesome deaths of others. He had imagined it, a thousand times or more – what had it been like for his father and what would it be like for him? But Turner saw that close combat was more brutal, more guttural, than anything he'd ever imagined. How could men do that to each other?

How could one man look in the face of another and then swing a club or jab a knife?

"I've failed in my first command," Turner said, more to himself than to the sergeant.

O'Keefe gave no response. He was holding up manfully, but he desperately wanted relief from the pain.

"They'll be needin' a bit of a payback, then, won't they?" O'Keefe said after a period of silence. "I won't speak for you, Lieutenant, but I'll not be leaving these mountains before I've gotten something for our boys who were killed."

Turner frowned, keeping his eye on the gulch below, making certain no threat had yet appeared.

"We'll get below, back to Del Norte, and send to the fort for help."

"Bah!" the Irishman spat back. "If we go back to Del Norte, they'll have time to escape. You go and get help. With a gun and a horse, I'll do me best to slow them down here."

"You'll go back with us, Sergeant, and I'll not discuss it anymore," Turner said, though he lacked much confidence in issuing an order. The troopers of his patrol almost all killed, Turner wasn't even sure that he had any authority to say a word to the sergeant. Perhaps, technically, he was still in command, but the reality was that he was hiding behind a rock, his sergeant could not walk, and it was Levi Stout who now made all the decisions for Turner's expedition.

As the two men sat in their perch, Turner's mind wandered to his father.

He had few clear memories of the man. The clearest

image of his father came from the stories he'd heard, and the story he'd most often imagined was the one of his father's death. Hooker was in charge of the Army of the Potomac and he'd taken his army across the Rappahannock River, establishing his headquarters east of the Army of Northern Virginia in a little crossroads town called Chancellorsville. Unknown to Hooker, Lee's army made a wide flanking maneuver, getting south and west of Hooker's army. The surprise was absolute. The Rebels charged from the woods into Hooker's flank, and the Union men rolled up like a carpet, fleeing down the highway to the headquarters.

It was on the first day of the battle, as Hooker's army attempted to counter the rout taking place on the flank. In the night, Captain Elliot Turner Sr. had led two companies of men into the fray. The men were not any kind of organized companies, they were the remnants of decimated companies collected along the way. They said he led from the front, Captain Turner did. Sword aloft with a shout, "Follow me!" He died bravely, they said. His body showed many wounds. A bullet to the hip appeared to have been what brought him down. Two bayonet wounds to the chest, probably while he was already down, ended his life. But there were other wounds, too. A shot to the leg, and witnesses said he kept charging. A graze to the ribs that did not slow him down. A bullet pierced his shoulder, but he did not stop advancing until he was shot in the leg. The advance he led was sufficient to allow some men to escape.

Captain Turner's lieutenant came to visit his son after the war, and it was he who gave the family the story. He spoke of admiration for the Captain's leadership, his gentleness and dedication to the men who served under him, his courage under fire.

What would Sergeant O'Keefe say about Lieutenant Turner, the son of the man who died at Chancellorsville?

Turner could hear the words now: "Gone, he was, when the attack came, nowhere to be found. His command slaughtered while the lieutenant hid in the branches of a tree."

The imagined words stung. They would not be delivered to a child – there was no child. Instead, O'Keefe's recollection would come at the court martial.

The waiting was agony. Sitting here among these rocks, just waiting while another man was out there risking his life.

It was that lieutenant who visited him when he was a child who handed Turner the gun he now had holstered on his belt. A cap-and-ball Colt Army that his father had carried in the war. His father's saber was back at the campsite. He'd dreamed of one day carrying his father's weapons into battle.

He had a Smith & Wesson Model 3 cartridge revolver, his issued gun, back with his gear. He also had a Winchester carbine. If he was armed with his issued guns, he could hold off a small army from this vantage. Even if he had just the revolver now, he could protect himself and the lieutenant. Why was he now armed with a cap-and-ball revolver that would, at best, keep them alive for only a few minutes? Was it pride, nostalgia, a childish desire to connect himself to his father's memory? If he was any kind of soldier, the cap and ball Colt would be back at Fort Garland in his footlocker – a keepsake, not an armament of war.

There in the rocks, Lieutenant Elliot Turner realized that he would deserve the harshest sentence the judges at his court martial could hand to him.

Movement down below suddenly caught his eye, and Turner drew back.

He saw now that Stout had been right – the predicted pursuit had turned up.

They had a man who looked like an Indian leading them, and he was following the tracks Stout had left in the snow. The other men followed behind the Indian, all of them on foot and carrying a variety of primitive weapons. Though Turner saw that many of them carried revolvers on their belts.

He held his breath as he watched the men moving down through the gulch. They followed Stout's trail, and from his vantage point, Lieutenant Turner did not think they ever questioned it. The men crossed the stream, stepping through the snow in the tracks Stout had left. They disappeared into the forest of cedar and pine. When they were gone, the lieutenant looked at his sergeant. The man looked pale.

"That was them," Turner said. "They've taken the bait. They followed Stout's trail into the woods."

"How many?" O'Keefe asked. "Was it all of them, or did they leave some behind?"

Turner let out a breath and shut his eyes. He hadn't counted them. Was there anything he could do right?

He would just have to wait now, wait for Levi Stout, and hope for the best.

- 9 -

Tommy Irons lost the trail in the trees. The snow was in patches here, some of it had never made it to the ground, caught instead in the canopy of evergreens. But the sun warmed it, and over days, with no fresh snow falling, had turned it to water that fell to the ground and seeped between and under the bed of brown needles, softening the ground. Here Tommy sought signs – broken needles mashed into the earth by a footfall, a heel or toe print in the mud. He found a smear of mud on a flat rock. That was a sign. He searched until he found a freshly broken pine branch. Farther along there was a bare spot where a rock the size of his fist was driven into the mud, and just ahead of the rock an impression that looked like a toe. These were the things Tommy Irons found that kept them moving, but seeking them out took time.

"There are plenty of signs," Tommy said to Lou Stallings. "They made no effort to cover their tracks. Either they hope to move faster than we do and outrun us or they want us to be able to track them."

"Why would they want us to track them?" Lou asked, suddenly suspicious.

"Maybe they're planning an ambush," Tommy said. "Maybe they just hope to run fast enough that it don't matter if we follow them."

"You said there were eleven of them when you saw them yesterday," Lou said.

"That's right. Eleven. Including the scout."

"Then there's only three out here, and one of them is injured," Lou replied. "That's not enough for an ambush. They're trying to outrun us."

Tommy Irons nodded. "Likely."

"Let's move faster," Lou said.

The thing Tommy Irons did not like was that he didn't see sign enough to suggest that more than one man had come through here. He was beginning to wonder if two of the men had holed up somewhere, hiding. Maybe the injured man and one of the others. He didn't like to say anything of his suspicions to Lou Stallings. Lou was a man who spoke before he thought, and he might make a bad mistake now if he knew that Tommy Irons suspected they were following just one man.

But Tommy was beginning to form his own conclusions.

Levi Stout was a good man, smart in the woods and the mountains, skilled at following a trail, adept at surviving. It might be just Levi's tracks he followed now, and if Stout had left the other two, he'd done it for good reason. He must have some plan to spoil the plot. Either Levi Stout intended to get to help – Del Norte, or maybe some mining camp that was still occupied – or he intended to get to horses and supplies and get those other two out. Tommy mulled these as he continued along, following the tracks. He wasn't at a run, but he was making good time through the woods. The tracks weren't easy to find, but they were definitely there for the finding. He walked quickly, sometimes jogging with just a glance at the ground for confirmation that he continued on the right way.

A broken twig right in the middle of a print in the soft earth.

On a slope of ground, someone had slipped and left a long mark in the mud.

A print in a patch of snow.

And then nothing. No sign. No tracks. No broken twigs or even a toe print in the snow. Tommy hurried along now, jogging faster for another thirty or forty yards through the dense forest, but he'd lost the trail. It had disappeared as if the man had sprouted wings and taken flight.

Tommy Irons stopped, and the men following him stopped, too.

His first thought was to look into the canopy. The tracks disappeared so suddenly that Tommy thought it was reasonable the man had shimmied up a tree and was hiding among the branches. Tommy even walked around with his head cocked back and his eyes toward the sky, but he saw nothing. Then he backtracked to the last sign he'd seen, and he searched from there for the next track. But he saw nothing that might point to where Levi Stout had gone. And now Tommy Irons was sure of it: Levi Stout had led them on a chase, purposefully leaving tracks sufficient to follow, and when Levi thought he'd led them far enough, he became like a bird and flew away.

"What's the matter, Tommy?" Lou asked.

"It's not right," Tommy had said, convinced enough now to speak his concerns.

"What's not right?" Lou asked, and Tommy heard the tension in his voice.

"He sprouted wings, Lou," Tommy Irons said. "I don't think the other two are with him. I think we've just been following Levi, and I think he's taken flight."

"What do you mean he sprouted wings?" Lou Stallings asked, his face turning red with anger.

"The tracks disappear. Levi left tracks for us to follow, and then he stopped leaving tracks."

"There must be something," Lou Stallings spat. "Whatever you say, he didn't grow wings. He walked out of here."

Tommy Irons grunted in agreement.

"Uh-huh," he said. "He walked out of here. But he walked out of here more carefully than he walked into here."

"So where has he gone?" Lou asked.

"If I had to guess, I'd say he's gone back to fetch a horse and his guns."

Lou caught his breath.

"Wells," he whispered, realizing that his friend might

be in trouble.

Tommy grunted again.

"Huh," he said. "Wells is probably already dead, Lou."

- 10 -

Levi Stout watched Tommy Irons from the trees across the gulch, and he silently thanked the Lord for his first bit of good luck.

To actually lay eyes on his pursuers was better fortune than Stout could have hoped for. They were just crossing the stream, still exposed at the bottom of the gulch. They had a long way to go yet, and though they were just across the gulch, heading into the woods and in easy rifle shot, they were far behind.

Stout did not move. Not a muscle twitches, not a hair in his mustache flickered in the light breeze. He wouldn't allow any movement of his body to give him away and ruin the work he'd done.

Tommy Irons.

It was a disappointment to Levi Stout to see Tommy Irons with this outfit. He'd scouted some with Tommy up north, and he'd liked Tommy pretty well. Worse, Tommy Irons was a good scout. He knew his business better than most. Tommy wouldn't miss anything. If there was a point where Levi gave himself away without realizing it, Tommy would find it. But for now, for the next little bit, Stout had some confidence that the men pursuing him would move deep into the evergreen forest and they would be busy hunting for a man who had escaped them and passed them by.

Seeing the men, too, gave Levi an opportunity to alter his plan. Knowing where the main body of pursuers was, Levi decided he could get the lieutenant and the wounded sergeant from their perch and take them with him as he went to fetch the supplies and horses.

He also knew what he would be facing. There'd been eighteen men in the initial attack. He'd killed two of them to rescue the sergeant. Including Tommy Irons, there were an even dozen following his trail. Back at the troopers' camp there would be four men, if they were still there. Maybe those four had gone on to meet up with others somewhere else. Either way, Levi Stout had some knowledge now of what to expect when he went to get a horse.

It would mean, too, not having to come all the way back here to the gulch once he had secured provisions and risk being caught by Tommy and that group.

"Lieutenant!" Stout called from the bottom of the cliff where he'd left Turner and O'Keefe. He was attempting to shout in a whisper, to avoid an echo that might alert

Tommy Irons or one of those others. When at last the lieutenant peered out over the ledge, Stout said, "It's Levi Stout. I'm coming up."

Turner scanned the horizon as the scout made his way up the crevice. "Have you already gotten horses?" he asked as Stout emerged over the ledge.

"Not yet," he said.

"They just came through, not a quarter of an hour ago," Turner said.

"I saw them," Stout responded. He was bent over the sergeant, looking at O'Keefe's leg.

"It would be a good idea to get you to a doctor as quick as we can," Stout said. He turned to the lieutenant now, "You'll have to help me tote him."

Elliot Turner had the look of a man who would fill out and be strong, but he still had the narrow frame of a young man. Fortunately, Sergeant O'Keefe was not particularly large, himself. With his leg wrapped in his suspenders, O'Keefe could hobble part of the way, supported by the other two men.

When they had the sergeant down from the cliff side, Stout said to Lieutenant Turner, "Can you make your way back to the campsite?"

"I can," Turner said confidently.

"You can find your way?" Stout repeated the question to be sure Turner understood his concern.

"I can, Mr. Stout," Turner said with some emphasis.

"I'm going ahead," Stout said. "We don't have much time. They've got a man with them who I know, a scout named Tommy Irons. He knows his business. He won't be fooled for long."

Lieutenant Turner supported the weight of the injured sergeant, and together the two of them set off in Stout's wake.

Watching Stout leave, Turner could not feel more useless. His shame in the loss of his command continued to be compounded by his relegation to makeshift ambulance. His future, as far as he could see it, appeared bleak. Lieutenant Turner found it almost impossible to focus on survival when he saw nothing worth surviving for.

***

The four men had rounded up eighteen saddled horses and brought them into the camp. Stout could see these were the horses they'd brought with them. Obviously, Tommy Irons and the men with him decided to go on foot, unsure of the terrain they'd have to cross in their pursuit. Probably they did not expect the pursuit to go particularly far.

The horses the troopers rode were nowhere to be seen, though Stout figured they probably had not gone far. These men who were with Tommy Irons had spooked the horses and chased them off, but the first clump of grass would have distracted the horses from what spooked them and stopped their flight. There was a valley not far beyond the evergreen forest where the soldiers had camped, and Stout expected he would find the cavalry's horses down in that valley.

What concerned him now was the four men left behind in the camp.

They had tied the bodies of the two men Stout had

killed to a couple of the horses, and even as Stout arrived in a hidden position outside the camp, they seemed to be in a state of indecision. Crouched behind a cedar tree, Levi Stout watched as the men continued a heated discussion that had clearly been going on for some time. He wished that he could hear them clearly, but from the snatches of conversation he was able to catch, they seemed to be arguing about staying at the camp or leaving. They also seemed to be talking about meeting up with another group from their party. Stout guessed that this was the group in pursuit of him, led by Tommy Irons, but something about the way they talked and gestured and the direction they looked as they argued about what to do next made Stout think that they were discussing whether or not they should meet up with yet another group.

But if they did not leave the campsite in the next couple of minutes, Stout knew he would have to press the issue.

He needed weapons, and he needed horses, and he needed them in a hurry if they were going to get back to Del Norte ahead of Tommy Irons and that bunch with him. Stout would have paid good money right now for a rifle. Tommy Irons and those others might be close enough to hear the report of a rifle, but with a good repeating rifle, Levi Stout could dispatch these four men and take three horses and be on the way to Del Norte in just a few minutes. Hell, he'd even take a pistol if someone came along and offered it.

Weighing his options as he watched the men debate what they intended to do next, Levi decided the only thing for it would be to rush them. Their hands were covered in the blood of the troopers Stout had led into the mountains, and the army scout wasn't about to have any qualms about taking their lives. He slid his big fighting knife from its scabbard and prepared himself to kill these four men.

He moved quietly along the outskirts of the camp, keeping himself out of view behind the cedar trees and tangled saplings, seeking out the best position from which to approach his prey. This wasn't much different than hunting deer or elk, though he wasn't concerned about which way the wind was blowing. Instead, Stout sought an approach that would limit sight. The closer he could get to these men without being seen, the better the opportunity he would have to strike fast and effectively.

Stout had confidence that he could take any two of them in a straight fight. These men were killers, no question, but Levi Stout was strong and fast and, maybe more important, he was a desperate man. He had to take two out of the fight right away, and he had to do it by surprise. Four tenderfoots, he could probably take on his own. But these men weren't tenderfoots.

They had eighteen horses, saddled and standing aimlessly within the campsite the troopers had used. The horses were ambivalent to everything around them, including Stout. The best approach would be to come at them through the tight herd of horses.

He touched them on the rumps as he moved through them, coming at the horses from behind. He did not want to startle a horse and alert the men to his presence. He moved easily, touching the horses as he came upon them. One blew and shook its head, but nothing that would grab the attention of these four men. As he neared, Stout could better hear their conversation.

"There ain't no point in heading back up to meet with Jacob," one of the men said. "He's on his way here. We might as well wait for Lou to come back here."

"That suits me fine, except that Lou said to go on and

meet with Jacob," another countered.

"How are we going to lead eighteen horses?" another said. "We'll have horses scattered from here to Jimtown Camp."

The men stood not five yards from the pack of horses, and Stout now was running out of horses to hide behind. Crouched below the withers of one horse, he decided to make his move.

Stout came out from behind the horses and one of the men saw him immediately. But the scout moved quickly, crossing the short distance in an instant with three big strides and a final leap. The blade of his knife was sharp as a razor. He held the knife downward in his fist.

The man who saw him twisted his face into an expression of surprise and confusion such that the other three now followed his gaze, twisting to face Stout. But it was too late for them to react.

Stout's right fist, clutching the grip of the knife, came up in a blur and smashed the first man in the side of the head. The man reeled and stumbled away. With the knife poised high, now, Stout came at the second man with a downward cut. It was brutal work, violent death cutting through the man from just below his sternum to his hip, and cutting him deep.

The knife stuck, and Stout had to wrench it free.

The other two weren't as slow to react as Stout had hoped. One of them went for his six-gun on his hip, and the other tried to wrap Stout up in a bear hug.

It was close fighting now, and confused. Levi Stout felt a heavy blow to the back of his head that stunned him, even as he jabbed up with the knife to try to free himself from the grasp of one who'd wrapped him up. Jab with the knife, two, three times. He felt the resistance against it and knew he'd cut into flesh. He jerked an elbow high and felt it crack against a chin. Now he was free, and he swung wildly with the knife to back away any effort to grab him again.

It was the first man he'd punched in the side of the head who'd hit him from behind. From somewhere the man had found a club, and he raised it up high now and swung it with force at Stout's face as the army scout turned toward the man. Stout brought up his left arm and blocked the swing, taking a painful blow to his forearm. Now he lunged forward with the knife and missed, but he and the man with the club both went down in a heap.

Close in like this, these others were not a match for Levi Stout. He'd learned his trade from the Pawnee scouts who enjoyed a fight. On the ground, the two men rolled and Stout found himself on top but without much advantage as the man held his right wrist in a strong grip. The scout brought his knee up with a crushing blow into the man's groin, and the strength in the grip foundered. Stout's knife found the man's side, and then struck it again. Blood flowed freely from the two wounds.

He'd felled two of them, now.

The first man he'd cut so thoroughly that he was out of the fight, desperately trying to hold his guts from spilling out of his open stomach.

This man on the ground below him was bleeding so much that his life was running out, numbered now in minutes or seconds.

But the man who'd wrapped him in a bear hug, he was bleeding and hurt, but he still had fight left in him.

And the one with the gun.

Stout heard the loud snap of a pistol report and expected to feel the punch of the bullet, but the shot missed him. He sprang to his feet, ready to throw himself at the armed man. But the man was staggered, a gruesome hole exposing bone and mangled tissue opened up on the side of his face. A second bark of a gun, and the man was knocked off his feet as a heavy .44 ball knocked him like a hammer to the chest. Stout spun around and saw Lieutenant Turner, the cap and ball Colt in his hand, a small puff of gray gunsmoke hanging in the air.

The other man, with three knife wounds in his stomach, held up his hands to surrender. He dropped to a sitting position on the ground. His side had lost and the fight was gone now.

***

"Jacob Stallings," the man said, his chin in his chest as he lifted his shirt to examine the wounds in his gut. "He's the man paying our wages. His brother Lou is the boss, really, but it's Jacob paying wages." He pressed his fingers against his stomach and the blood came more freely.

"Damn," he muttered. "I think I'm killed."

Stout looked at the man's wounds. The other three were dead. The one Turner shot was killed by the second shot. The one Stout stabbed in the side, he'd bled out already. And the first man Stout cut, with his guts spilling, was on his back on the ground in a merciful delirium brought on by blood loss and shock from the horror of his condition.

"You're in a bad spot," Stout said. "I've seen Tommy Irons dress and stitch a gunshot wound. Maybe he can do something for you."

"You know Tommy?" the man asked, catching his breath as a wave of pain hit him as he spoke.

"I scouted for the army with Tommy Irons," Stout said. "So Jacob Stallings – he planning a claim jump? Is that what all this is about?"

"That's the size of it," the man said.

It did not strike Levi Stout as odd that he could now converse openly with this man he'd just fought – this man he'd just fought and probably killed. A dying man with no fight left in him has nothing left to lie for.

"Stallings works for a mining company. They pay him to prospect, and his deal gives him a cut of anything the company pulls out of the ground. It's a rich claim he's got now."

Stout nodded. He was growing impatient for the lieutenant's return. He didn't need to hear any more from this man. He understood all he needed to about this business and what had taken place and why. Now he just needed Lieutenant Turner to get back with Sergeant O'Keefe. The lieutenant had left O'Keefe in the woods and hurried forward to see what he could do to help Stout. It was a lucky decision, the scout decided, for the lieutenant had probably prevented Stout from getting shot in the back.

Importantly, Stout and the lieutenant had collected arms. Stout armed himself with his own Model 3 six-shooter and also tucked one of the troopers' Model 3s into his belt. He also had his repeating rifle held casually in his crossed arms as he talked to the man on the ground.

Lieutenant Turner had set aside his cap-and-ball Colt in favor of his own Smith and Wesson Model 3. He did not tote a rifle as he went back to get O'Keefe.

"What's your name?" Stout said.

"Phil Wells."

"Do you have people you want me to write to?"

Wells shrugged.

"I've got a sister in Kansas, but there ain't no point in writing. I haven't talked to her in years. She's probably done been thinking I was dead. Lou Stallings is probably the closest thing I've got to family. Me and him have been friends for a long time."

Stout shrugged his shoulders.

There was no point going in search of the cavalry horses, not when minutes might mean the difference between living and dying. They would take three of these saddled horses and start for Del Norte as soon as Lieutenant Turner and Sergeant O'Keefe got back. Stout was concerned that Tommy Irons and those others might have heard the two shots from Turner's gun, and those men in pursuit would likely give up trying to follow tracks and hurry back here now. Probably, Phil Wells would be dead by the time they got to him.

"It's a hard world sometimes," Stout said. "I'm sorry for you, Wells."

"We all make our choices," Wells said. "My choices brought me here. Help me over to that clearing where I can see the mountains. If I'm going to lay here and die, I might as well have something to look at."

- 11 -

"Was that a gunshot?" someone asked.

Lou Stallings held up a hand to shush the men in his outfit. They all heard the second shot, and there was no mistaking it.

"Oh, hell," Lou said. "They've got around behind us. They're back where we left Phil and the others."

Without a word from Lou or Tommy Irons, the men began turning and heading back. Some went at a run, their rifles held out in front of them to block branches from whipping them in the face. Others set off at a jog, knowing they were still a good distance away. Lou Stallings was among those running, though he knew that if things had gone bad for Phil Wells and the others, he was going to be too damn late to do anything to change that.

They scattered out through the woods now, the dozen men, leaping fallen trees and jumping between the thick growth of cedar trees. Three or four of them outpaced the others by quite a bit, getting twenty, thirty yards ahead of the others. Then they were farther than that. Lou Stallings tried to keep up with these men, but he couldn't do it. Lou was no runner. Most of the time, if he was going to get anywhere on foot, he would get there by walking, and if he was going to get anywhere fast, he was going to get there on horseback.

All the men jogged or ran and did what they could to keep up with those in the front, except one.

Tommy Irons stood for several moments while the others chased through the forest. He watched their backs. Ten men, not including Lou Stallings, who looked to get a couple of hundred dollars for what they were doing. They'd killed an outfit of prospectors, killed a cavalry patrol, and now they were hunting the survivors. To Tommy Irons, it seemed small wages for so much trouble, with a promise of more trouble to come.

So Tommy waited as the others ran on through the woods, and when they had gone from sight, only then did he begin to follow. He went at a walk, nothing more than a stroll through the woods.

Soon the dash through the woods devolved as the men realized they had already come farther than they could any of them run, and those who led at the start began to follow behind. So Lou Stallings soon found himself in the front of his men again, and Lou did better than most at keeping up a fast pace. He took long strides when he could not jog, and he stopped running before he was so spent that he had to pause to catch his breath. When he could, he would sprint ahead, or jog a ways.

He came out of the forest overlooking the little stream down in the narrow bottom of the gulch, and instinctively his eyes scanned the cliffs on the opposite side of the gulch.

Now he saw that there were so many places where a man might hide – the crevices leading up the sandstone, the cliffs above, the huge boulders and outcroppings down below. How easy it would have been for someone to plant a false trail to lead them the wrong direction and then hide there in those cliffs. But he did not linger. Instead, he hurried down the slope toward the spring and then back up the other side.

Stallings bent double going back up the slope of the gulch. He was exhausted and having trouble now catching his breath. None of the other men fared much better, struggling against the slope as they followed Lou. And then they were back in among the trees, following the route they'd initially taken earlier in pursuit of the three cavalrymen who escaped. When at last Stallings broke through the cedar trees into the clearing where the troopers had camped and where they had died, he saw immediately that there'd been trouble.

Their horses were all picketed in the clearing, but not saddled. The two men who'd been killed in the initial assault on the troopers were lashed to their horses.

"Phil!" Lou called as he started to walk through the campsite, and then he saw why the horses were not saddled. The straps had been cut on all the saddles. Now Lou Stallings knew for sure that Phil Wells and the three he'd kept back with him had encountered dire trouble.

And then Lou spotted the dead men – the bodies of three of the four he'd left behind. One of them flayed open in brutal fashion. Another one laying in a patch of red snow, and a third shot in the face and chest. But he did not see Phil Wells.

The others with Phil were beginning now to filter into the camp and could see for themselves what had occurred here.

"They got in behind us, Lou," one of the men commented.

"I can see that for myself," Lou said, angry as he looked about for Phil Wells.

Another, looking at the troopers' saddles, called out, "They've cut the straps on these, too."

"Don't matter," Lou said. "We can ride bareback if we have to. What matters is that we get after them. They'll be headed down the trail for Del Norte, now. And where in hell is Tommy Irons?"

"Hey, boss," one the men called to Lou. It was Dicky Cort calling to him from below a tall ponderosa pine at the edge of a wide clearing overlooking the valley below. Dicky had helped Lou and Phil Wells put together this outfit. He'd brought in five or six of the men. Hassled and frustrated to no end, Lou Stallings marched over to where Dicky Cort was standing, and on the other side of the ponderosa pine, facing the mountains, Lou saw Phil Wells' body. He was laid out on a horse blanket with one of the troopers' blankets over him to keep him warm. Dicky reached down and pulled away the blanket, and the two men saw where Phil's clothes were stiff with blood around the stab wounds.

"Damn," Lou said.

The men moved quickly to rig up saddles, using rope to replace the cut cinches. Lou Stallings found he again had to split his party. He detailed four of the eleven men left to him to cart off the bodies of the men from their outfit – Phil and the others.

"Find a place to bury them," Lou instructed the men. "Somewhere where nobody will find them. Then go and find my brother and tell him we've had a disaster. I'm taking the others and we're going after these three to try to get them before they reach Del Norte."

He looked around one last time for Tommy Irons, but Tommy had disappeared. The last anyone saw of him was when they heard the gunshots. Right now, Lou Stallings needed Tommy Irons to be here helping him track these men. But Tommy wasn't anywhere around, and that was one more thing that worried Lou.

Lou Stallings cast his gaze across at the western mountains that had been Phil Wells' last sight of this earth. It was already getting late into the afternoon. There was small chance that he could catch these three cavalrymen before dark, but it would take them three or four days to get to Del Norte. That was plenty of time to stop them.

- 12 -

"It's three days, maybe four, to get back to Del Norte," Levi Stout said, looking at the sun already low over the tops of the mountains to the west. They only had maybe four hours left of daylight. "The snow is melted some since we come out, so the trail out won't be as bad as the trail in. But it's still distance, and the horses can only go so hard for so long."

They'd had another bit of luck. On the ride out, they came across a half dozen of the cavalry horses grazing down in the valley. They cut out three of the horses, allowing each of them to have a spare mount. A spare horse for each man meant they could drive the horses at a trot longer and then switch horses. It meant riding through the night, shortening the length of time to get back to Del Norte from three days to two, maybe. They were changing mounts now after an hour or so of hard riding.

"Anything can happen in three days," Lieutenant Turner said. "Those men can disappear in three days."

"They can at that," O'Keefe agreed.

"It won't matter if they do," Stout said. "I have their names. Lou Stallings. Jacob Stallings. We can swear warrants in Del Norte and put the law on them."

"They attacked a patrol of U.S. Cavalry," Turner said. "It should be up to the U.S. Cavalry to go after them."

"And the U.S. Cavalry will go after them, Lieutenant," O'Keefe said. "Rest assured of that. When we get to Del Norte, we'll send to Fort Garland for a company of men."

"There's no telegraph lines," Lieutenant Turner said. "We'll have to send a rider. That's another three or four days. At best, we're looking at a week before we can get a company of men."

"We can round up a posse in Del Norte," Stout said, his voice low and betraying his frustration. They'd covered good ground since getting mounts, but Stout felt certain that the pursuit would renew quickly. Cut saddle straps would only delay the men so long. "Don't forget, Lieutenant Turner, whatever else these men did, they killed an outfit of prospectors to jump their claim. I guarantee there will be plenty of men wintering in Del Norte who will volunteer for that posse."

As the three men talked, Turner took a look at O'Keefe's injured leg. The sergeant was in bad shape. He needed to get to a doctor, he needed the wound to be cleaned out and stitched up. The man was in obvious pain, but he bore it manfully. Turner now wrapped the leg in bandages.

"You've got to get to a doctor," Turner said. "Is there a doctor in Del Norte?"

"Oh, sure," O'Keefe said. "Some sawbones from the war, probably on the morphine, but steady enough hands for a job like this."

Turner had already made up his mind, and all the discussion with Stout was useless. He would give the man an order – probably the last he would ever issue – and that would be the end of the conversation. Lieutenant Turner was in no mood to debate with a subordinate.

"I'm going to stay back," Turner announced, tying off the bandage and then standing to face Stout as he tightened the cinch on his saddle.

"That's a poor notion, Lieutenant," O'Keefe said. "Come back to Del Norte with us and let's gather up a posse."

"Mr. Stout, you get Sergeant O'Keefe to Del Norte. You send word of what's happened to Fort Garland, and you work with the local law to form up a posse."

Stout narrowed his eyes at the man, his face stolid.

"What exactly do you intend to do, Lieutenant Turner?" Stout asked.

"I'll conceive a delaying action to stall their retreat out of these mountains. I'll buy you time to get a posse together and rejoin me."

"Ah, Lieutenant Turner," O'Keefe said. "A short action it would be. They've got a passel of men, Lieutenant, and you're naught but one."

"If I can delay them and give you time to get back to Del Norte –" Lieutenant Turner began, but Levi Stout cut him off.

"We're running out of time here, Lieutenant. You're talking about delaying them, but I don't think you appreciate how small the chance is that the three of us will be able to get back to Del Norte. Those men are determined killers, and we've got a wounded man. There's a second party of them, too, and we don't know where they might be."

"What makes you think so?" Turner asked.

"I talked to that man, Wells, and he said their outfit is led by two brothers. One was chasing us, and the other was breaking down their camp at the claim. The other brother is still out here, and we don't know where. It's best that we just keep going."

Turner shook his head.

"I've made up my mind," he said. "You get Mr. O'Keefe back to Del Norte. Get a posse together. Get word back to the fort."

Stout started to speak again, but Turner raised up a hand.

"No, Mr. Stout. I'll brook no more argument. I'm issuing you an order."

Stout bristled.

As an army scout who came and went as he pleased, Stout took wages but wasn't enlisted in the army, and as such he wasn't much accustomed to taking orders from anyone other than Faustina.

"I have their names, Lieutenant," Stout said. "Jacob Stallings. Lou Stallings. Even if we cannot catch them now, we can get warrants."

"That's not good enough, Mr. Stout. If I don't delay them, they'll be able to get down below and scatter. They'll change their names and disappear. You know it's true, Stout. These men slaughtered my command. I'm going to do everything I can to delay their escape and make certain they come to justice."

Levi Stout looked at Sergeant O'Keefe for support, but the Irishman sat mute on the ground where Turner had bandaged his leg.

"You won't delay them," Stout said. "But you'll get yourself killed. You're better off helping me and the sergeant get below to Del Norte. We can send to Fort Garland, notify the law. We can get up a posse to meet these men as they ride out of the mountains. But if you stay back, you'll get yourself killed."

"Get Mr. O'Keefe to Del Norte," Turner said. "Then do the other things. I'll buy you time to get below, and I'll delay these men as long as I can."

Turner now slid a foot into the stirrup and swung himself up into the saddle. He wheeled the horse around and then twisted around and looked back at the scout and the cavalry sergeant.

"Go, Mr. Stout. Mr. O'Keefe needs a doctor and we need to get word to town."

***

Sergeant O'Keefe drove the three spare horses in front of him. Levi Stout rode just behind.

"That boy's going to get himself killed," Stout said.

They'd maintained a good lope along the worn trail leading back to Del Norte. In places where it drifted and blew and piled high, the snow remained along the sides of the road, especially in the shadows of the tall cedar trees. But the road was mostly clear of snow now, and though the mud slowed them in places, the horses had level, soft ground that made for easy going. Stout suggested they'd get farther faster if they kept the horses at long lopes rather than short gallops.

"Likely he will," O'Keefe agreed. The man's voice was tinged with pain, and Stout could see the sergeant was struggling. "But he's not got much prospect if he comes with us. It'll be a court-martial, and a poor outcome for the lieutenant."

Stout grunted.

Just then, O'Keefe reined up. Stout rode ahead, passing him by, and brought his horse to a gallop to overtake the three spare horses. He easily turned them and brought them back to O'Keefe.

"Sorry," O'Keefe said, gingerly swinging his injured leg over the saddle and then stepping down onto the ground. He leaned heavily against the horse. "The leg's playing hell rubbing against the side of the horse."

O'Keefe bit his lip and winced as he tried to put some weight on the leg. The sergeant took a step away from the horse, making for a rock that he hoped to sit on, and he stumbled and almost lost his balance. He cursed loudly as he caught himself with the bad leg, sending a lightning shock of pain up his leg and into his head. Stout dropped from the saddle and hurried over to the man to help him to the rock.

"Not sure what we'll do," O'Keefe said. "I can't keep going like this, and we can't outrun them if we slow down."

Stout thought of Faustina, back home and preparing for winter. She'd be preserving fruit, maybe riding the buggy into town for a little more flour and coffee beans to see them through. There was wood enough to get her through the winter in comfort, and they had vegetables in the root cellar and meat in the smokehouse. She would get through the winter. And come spring, well.

"She's a good woman," Levi Stout said, giving voice to his thoughts.

"What's that, then?" O'Keefe asked.

Stout grunted.

"Nothing," he said. "My wife lives in the village of San Luis, south Fort Garland. We've got a little cabin in town there. If I don't make it out of this, go to her and let her know. She's a good woman. She'll be angry at me for getting myself killed, but go to her and let her know."

"What are you talking about?" O'Keefe asked, narrowing his eyes.

Stout clenched his jaw and shook his head, a heavy breath from his nose rustling the whiskers of his mustache. He seemed to be wrestling with something, some idea, so O'Keefe gave him a moment. But in truth, the sergeant already knew what was in Stout's mind.

"The lieutenant had the right idea," Stout said. "What's important is that we have to get word back to Del Norte. You'll have to ride through the night to stay ahead of them, but you've got spare mounts. You don't need me to help you. Just keep riding."

"You don't have to go back," O'Keefe said. "We can both ride through the night. The lieutenant made his decision."

Stout shrugged.

"Those men are going to be determined to catch stop us from getting to Del Norte. I reckon they'll come on pretty hard and fast. Even riding through the night, you might not be able to stay ahead of them. But if the lieutenant and I can slow them down." Stout left the thought unfinished. "Anyway, I'm riding back to join the lieutenant. And I'm asking you, Sergeant O'Keefe – her name is Faustina. Like I said, she's a good woman. She'll take it hard, but I'd be obliged if you would go and see her, if I don't make it out of this, and let her know that she was in my final thoughts."

The Irish being generally a sentimental race, and O'Keefe being an Irishman to the marrow, he couldn't help but agree.

"I'll go and see your woman, you can rest assured of that," O'Keefe promised.

Stout nodded his thanks to the man and then climbed back into his saddle.

"Good luck, Sergeant."

"And to you," O'Keefe said with a nod.

The sergeant rested a few minutes more. He wrapped another bandage around his leg to give him a little extra protection against the horse's side.

- 13 -

Finding himself alone, mounted atop his horse, Elliot Turner experienced an epiphany.

At West Point he had heard so many lectures on tactical advantages and "good ground," but he'd never before truly swept his eye across a piece of terrain and sought to find in it an advantageous position. But now, with the river ambling over its rocky bed on his left shoulder and the towering sandstone cliffs on either side, he realized just what it meant to capture and hold the high ground.

From the right position, he would be as if in an impenetrable fortress. The craggy rocks would be like his battlements. The approach up the cliffs would be his moat. He had two boxes of shells for the Winchester rifle. The lieutenant imagined himself holed up in a secure position, firing down upon his attackers until they were all eliminated. The valley would be his killing field. All he had to do was find the right spot – a place where he could climb but would be difficult to reach for men under fire, a place that gave him a vantage of the valley but would be nearly impossible to shoot into, a place where he could hole up overnight if it came to that. And so his eyes continued to search the landscape above him as he rode along on the horse.

And then his gaze lit on the spot.

The slope of the hill was gentle and rounded, but near the precipice, the solid rock escarpments seemed to stretch straight up into the sky. Eight or ten feet up the escarpment there was a rocky outcropping that created a ledge. Boulders surrounding the ledge gave it the natural battlements he was looking for. That hill would slow any man trying to get up on it, exposing them to fire from a man on the ledge, and other than a few scattered cedar trees and a few large boulders, there was no natural cover to protect anyone who was attempting a charge at the ledge. The climb to the ledge was not great, but it was a straight-up, hand-over-hand climb and would give anyone defending that ledge a final advantage if it came to the last moment.

Turner gave the horse some leg, directing him toward the hill. Ahead, a small grouping of short cedar trees gave the perfect place to tie the horse and keep him out of sight from anyone approaching from the west. Turner made for there first. He would unsaddle the horse, picket him behind the trees, and then take his saddlebags with provisions and ammunition and set himself up on the ledge. It would prove to be the perfect position. Even if they got in behind him, Turner saw no easy approach that would allow his adversaries to get above him without exposing themselves.

The lieutenant felt a sense of victory already. His education had paid off, and if he managed to subdue a much greater force, he might yet snatch some small bit of glory from defeat. Already in his mind the court martial was taking on a very different shape than the one he had earlier anticipated. A formality. An opportunity for congratulations, perhaps even promotion. Though he had faced an overwhelming force and lost his command, he had managed to turn defeat into triumph.

Promotion might be too much to expect, but Turner believed now he had found a way to at least avoid disgrace.

That's when he heard the rifle shot shatter the silence of the countryside and echo and answer back from the surrounding cliffs. The horse stumbled, and Turner dragged the reins to pull its head back up. But it stumbled forwards a second time, and then there was another burst of gunfire – three or four rifle shots, booming loud. The lieutenant found himself startled from his thoughts and, for a moment, unable to even comprehend what was happening. He'd not yet connected the stumbling horse to that first gunshot.

Now the horse seemed to catch his second wind, and he started to bound forward, and Turner realized the animal must have been shot just as the forelegs surrendered and the great beast seemed to buckle and drop head first. The lieutenant, with the agility of a young man, threw himself clear of the falling horse and landed hard on the rocky soil.

Now the gunshots began in earnest, bullets chipping

rock all around him.

Turner laid flat for a moment, and then looked at his killed mount. Disaster has struck just as he'd discovered a path to success.

Turner pushed himself from the ground and leapt back toward the horse. He saw now that the horse had been shot at least twice, once in the breast and a second time on the left from shoulder. That first shot must have been fatal. They'd brought him down like one would a buffalo.

He had to work to pry the Winchester out from under the horse and get it loose of the saddle. He could not easily get the saddlebags from under the horse's weight, so he opened up the one free bag and reached inside. He came back out with a box of bullets, and a second time his hand emerged with a small portion of jerky.

Even as he felt around inside the saddlebag, the lieutenant scanned the distant tree line for the source of the shots. They were not difficult to find. Just inside the trees, a dozen men had taken up positions. White gunsmoke against the dark of the woods readily gave away their position, and even as he watched, Lieutenant Turner could see men moving within the tree line to try to get at a better position. Between him and them, there was ample open ground that prevented the men from making a dash. Any of those men could see that a well-worked rifle could make that distance insurmountable for at least some among their numbers.

Turner clutched the box of shells and the jerky in his hand and took a deep breath, as if about to plunge into a swimming hole, and then he sprang up, making a run for the position on the ledge.

***

Levi Stout's thoughts remained with his wife in San Luis as the horse galloped back over ground where it had recently passed.

It was a simple fact that a man with a little knowledge, a strong back, and a lot of determination could survive on his own in this harsh world out West. He could cut the timber, shoot and clean the game, patch the roof, stoke the fire, smoke the meat, fetch the water, and get through one winter after the other if he had to. And if worse came to worst, he could always go and find a job mucking stalls at a livery, pouring drinks at a saloon, punching cattle on a ranch, or any other number of jobs. This was, in every way, a man's world where the right sort of man could not only survive, but he could thrive. Nature set up like this. If God didn't intend for men to do well in this world, he wouldn't have made the mountains so big, the winter months so long, the ground covered in rocks and cactus, nor would he have made the rattlesnakes as big around as a thigh. God didn't intend for this to be country for women and children.

A woman, to survive here, needed a man. She'd have to be an uncommon woman to make it on her own through more than one or two harsh winters of the San Luis valley. And it was a simple fact of life that most women who found themselves on their own in the West soon learned just how much of a man's world it was. How many widows turned to whoring just to be able to feed themselves and their children? Stout knew of too many to make him happy with his decision to go back to the lieutenant.

Faustina's best hope now was that she'd get through this winter and come spring a decent man would come along who would treat her well. It wasn't a happy thought for Levi Stout, to think of her with another man. But that's what he was, when he got right down to it. Stout considered himself a decent man who'd come along and found a widow on the verge. He'd married her and given her a hope for the future, and in the past couple of years they'd built a life together. Faustina had security, and Stout had a woman who cared whether he came home. Her best hope, if a bullet should take him out here in the mountains, would be for a decent man to come along. But a twice-over widow might scare some men off, thinking she's cursed.

They were absurd thoughts, Stout decided, especially for a man who was likely riding to his own death.

And that was the thought hanging in his head when he heard from not far up ahead the report of a rifle. Stout sat back in the saddle and drew the reins. The horse slowed but with a head of steam he did not stop, but instead danced a circle or two, his legs still going even as Stout drew back harder on the reins.

And then came a volley, a thundering of shots, echoing against the sandstone walls surrounding the river valley.

Stout slid his rifle from its scabbard, cinched to the saddle, and dropped the lever to chamber a round.

Whatever was going to happen was coming soon.

- 14 -

Jacob Stallings came down from the claim late in the afternoon. He expected to meet up with his brother, but when he arrived at the campsite where the soldiers had been slaughtered, the men his brother had left behind told him what had occurred there.

He hurried them along, not concerned the way Lou had been about whether or not they left evidence that might suggest the massacre of the soldiers had been something other than an attack by Utes angry over the encroachment onto their territory. When he heard that three of the soldiers had survived the attack and gotten away, Jacob Stallings began to panic. The men were in their saddles and riding quickly in Lou's wake. Jacob was desperate to catch his brother before dark, desperate before the close of day to hear that the problem had been solved.

Jacob rode on ahead with a couple of the others, leaving behind those who were leading the horses with the dead bodies of their killed men, including Phil Wells. And though he rode hard, he had not caught up with Lou before he heard the gunshots ahead. It was difficult to determine down in the valley, with the echoes and the confusion of multiple rifles being fired at once, but Jacob figured the shots were still a couple of miles away. So he spurred on his horse. Surely those gunshots had to be Lou and the others.

So Jacob rode hard, covering ground quickly and now even leaving behind those who had managed to keep up with him.

The valley trail – a trail followed by generations of Utes and other Indians who had made these mountains home far before any European even knew these mountains existed – dipped down close to the river, skirting the edge of a wide swath of cedars and pines intermingled with patches of quaking aspens. As he rounded a bend in the trail that followed along beside a bend in the river, Jacob saw up ahead several saddled horses picketed with a couple of men keeping watch over them. He still heard gunshots ahead, though it was just a smattering of rifle fire now. Jacob drove his horse toward the men and horses, and he recognized two of his men.

He didn't have their names. They were all Joe and Tommy and Will and whatever else to him. Necessary pieces for Jacob Stallings to get what he wanted, but not interesting enough for him to engage them in conversation or get to know any of them personally.

Almost the only one in the outfit Jacob really talked to was his brother Lou. He knew Phil Wells, of course – Phil, now tied to a horse back behind. He knew a couple of the others by name, but only because they'd worked with Lou for so long.

"Where's my brother?" Jacob demanded, riding up to the men.

"Through them woods there," one of the men said, casting his head in the direction of the gunfire. "It's hot in there, though. You might be best to wait here."

"Have you caught the soldiers who escaped?" Jacob asked.

The man chuckled, and so did the other, and their buffoonery only heightened Jacob's agitation.

"They caught something, I'd say. If it's a rabbit, they're laying down a surprising rate of fire."

"What the hell does that mean?" Jacob said, swinging himself out of the saddle and then stumbling as his first foot hit the ground. His legs had gone numb in the saddle.

"It means I reckon they're shooting at them soldiers," the man grumbled.

Jacob handed off his reins to the man and started through the woods, following the sound of the shots. As the booming of the rifles became louder and sharper, Jacob Stallings dropped into a crouch. He did not know what he'd find up ahead, but if the soldiers were shooting back, he did not want a stray bullet to find its way to him.

Through the trees up ahead he saw daylight, and there he found men huddled behind the trunks of the big ponderosa pines. Among them, standing more exposed than Jacob would have liked, he saw his brother Lou. Now

Jacob hurried toward him.

"What the hell is going on?" Jacob asked.

Lou jumped, startled by the sudden appearance of his younger brother. He took a big breath and let it out in a heavy sigh and tossed up his hands in a gesture of regret.

"Here, step away," Lou said as one of the men standing nearby fired a shot that deafened them both momentarily.

The brothers walked back through the trees, slipping through the branches of a couple of firs, and when they found themselves enough sheltered from the sound of the gunshots to communicate Lou Stallings again held up his hands in a regretful gesture.

"We attacked them soldiers just after dawn, like you and me said," Lou told his brother. "Somehow, and I don't know how, three of them got away. I'm guessing maybe they were a little outside of the campsite, but in the process, they killed two of our men."

The body count wasn't important to Jacob Stallings, and he shrugged it off as Lou gave him the details.

"We tracked them, but they managed to get around behind us," Lou said. "I'd left Phil Wells to clean up the mess, and those soldiers came in and killed Phil and the men I'd left with him. That's six of our men they took out this morning."

"So you've got the three of them trapped now?" Jacob asked.

"Not exactly, no. As we were following the trail here, we saw one of them riding back toward us. Just the one. Dicky Cort put down his horse, and he scrambled up that hill and into that cliff face yonder."

Jacob looked, but they'd gone back deep enough in the woods that he could no longer see down the trail.

"Just the one?" Jacob asked.

"Just the one," Lou said. "I told the boys to keep it hot on him, and we've sent several volleys at him. But so far, it don't look like anything has took."

"This is damned consternating," Jacob said. "What about the other two?"

Lou did his helpless gesture again.

"I can't go after the other two until I've dealt with the one," he said.

"Send some of the men ahead, then, and keep others behind," Jacob snarled. "We've got to get this dealt with."

"From his vantage, he's got a range on a good length of the trail. If he's any kind of marksman, he'd be able to hit anyone who tried to skirt past him."

Jacob Stallings had no choice but to defer to his brother. This was his brother's line, and not his.

"We lost Tommy Irons," Lou said.

For Jacob Stallings, this was another blow. Though he didn't have much use for the other men, Jacob had employed Tommy Irons as a guide many times and he valued the man. He'd long thought that if anything ever happened to Lou, Tommy Irons would make a decent replacement.

"They killed Tommy?"

"No," Lou said. "Tommy just disappeared. I think he's run out on us."

Jacob felt helpless. For a man who preferred to be in control of everything, the present situation seemed completely outside of his command. None of his skills or knowledge would be useful in a gunfight, and he did not understand how one man was holding off a dozen.

The two men pushed their way back through the cedar trees, and just as they did, a rifle barked from where the soldier was hiding on the cliff, and a man standing not fifteen yards in front of the Stallings brothers doubled over and fell into a tree.

"Damn," Lou Stallings said, rushing forward to see if he could help the man.

- 15 -

Elliot Turner had not fired a shot.

When the men in the trees unhorsed him, Turner collected what he could from his saddlebags and then made a dash for the hillside.

They lost him behind the stand of cedar trees, so he kept running. The shooting from the trees resumed, and he dove behind a boulder too small to completely shelter him. A shot, or a ricochet, or a rock chipped by a bullet scraped along the sole of his boot, and that was enough to get the lieutenant moving again. Without thinking, he ran for the place he'd already had in mind as a stronghold. When he got there, he found a crevice in the rock just wide enough for him to squeeze into. He managed to wedge his way up that crevice to a foothold where he pushed and pulled and prodded himself up to the ledge he'd intended to use as cover for his ambush.

Every few minutes three or four of the men in the woods let loose a volley that chipped rock all around him, but he found himself perfectly safe behind the rocks that formed the ledge. The rocks enough resembled parapets that he was also able to watch as the men took up positions. They worked their way along the tree line as far as they could and they had him covered from the front and the side. He could not make an escape from the ledge, but they also could not get past him along the trail.

His gambit paid off. He'd found a position from which he could buy time for Stout and O'Keefe. Even if it was just the hour or so before dark fell, it was something – some sort of redemption for his lost command.

Now he had to give those men inside the tree line something to consider before they attempted to advance.

Turner slid his carbine up between a couple of rocks, and then he raised up so that he was on his knees.

At West Point, the lieutenant had been something of a marksman. He'd hunted deer with his uncle many times as a child, and on those occasions shot an old flintlock rifle. He'd learned, then, to be accurate in his aim before pulling a trigger.

Now he found a target standing beside a pine tree. The man had just enough light behind him, seeping through the canopy of trees, that his silhouette made a perfect target. Turner leaned into the gun just a touch, taking a firm grip on the fore stock, looking down the sights. He targeted the man's torso. Turner didn't much care where the bullet struck, whether the wound was mortal or even if it took him permanently out of the fight. What mattered most for Turner was that he hit his target and gave those men something to think about. If the first shot he fired hit a man, maybe Turner could unnerve some of the others.

He squeezed the trigger and watched the silhouette double over and then fall forward into the tree. Through the dark woods, Turner could see a man rushed to the fallen man, and then another.

All his targets immediately disappeared, though. There'd been several silhouettes among the trees, men who were careless because their foe had made no effort to get at them. Now that they knew he intended to shoot back, though, they'd all ducked low to the ground or been more careful about positioning themselves behind trees. Where he'd had five or six good targets, Turner now saw none.

A grayness began to permeate the air, and Turner knew this was darkness coming. The sun was gone now, dipping below the mountains. It lit the sky, but dusk was upon them. Soon it would be pitch black out, and in the darkness all of the advantages of Turner's fortification would disappear. They'd be able to get at him, and there was little he could do about it other than to put his back against the cliff wall and shoot at any shadow he saw.

***

The gunfire tapered off as Levi Stout neared the sound, but there were still enough shots being fired that he knew when he was close enough that he had to be careful about being seen. So he dropped out of the saddle and took the horse into a stand of trees. Stout had no idea how soon he might return, or even if he would return, so he tied the horse to the trunk of a pine on a long line, giving him plenty of room to forage.

The scout put a box of shells for his rifle and some jerky into his possibles bag, and then he started making his way up the side of the hill over near the steep sandstone cliffs. He thought the shooting was coming from just beyond the hill, and here he had a few trees and rocks from which he could hide behind to cover his approach to the fight. He had no idea what he would find up ahead, though he expected that the lieutenant had ambushed the Stallings outfit. The hillside followed the curve of the river, and he had to make his way around a large curve before he heard a sharp report from a rifle. He was close now. The other shots he'd heard had been muffled by distance and the hills, but that most recent shot was clear and close by.

And then Stout saw the dead horse down on the trail. He recognized it immediately as the horse the lieutenant had been riding. But he took heart that the lieutenant was not there with the horse, either wounded or pinned down in a precarious position by gunfire.

The shooting had now stopped, but it was anything but quiet. Stout heard shouting coming from the woods. The wind rattled and moaned as it blew through the tops of the pines, rustled the branches of the firs, and tittered what leaves remained on the aspens. And the air was heavy, too, with the tension of a gunfight. Stout's nose curled against the bitter smell of expended gunpowder.

He pressed himself up close to the sandstone wall, making his way slowly and trying as best he could to stay hidden.

Stout wedged himself into a crevice when a volley

burst from the woods, but he realized immediately their target was well in front of his position. He stretched his neck, trying to see without being seen, and found the place where he thought the lieutenant must've holed up. It appeared to be a good position, defensible and with a commanding view of the trail below.

Stout found a place where he could stay hidden from the men in the woods up ahead, and there he took a seat. He feared if he tried to get closer to the lieutenant that he would be seen.

The dead horse worried him. It was possible that Turner had been injured and was in trouble in his position. It might be that the man needed help right now and maybe couldn't wait much longer. But Stout did not think he'd do any good if he went forward now. If he exposed himself, he probably would succeed only in getting himself killed.

They were not long until dark overcame them. Stout decided he would make a move to get to the lieutenant in the dark.

- 16 -

Levi Stout wrapped his fingers around the grip of his knife when he heard voices in the darkness.

He'd waited what had to be close to three hours beyond full dark to start to make his move toward the ledge where lieutenant Turner was hunkered down, and when he finally did begin to move, he went very slowly. He could stumble and kick loose a rock or he could trip over a branch or a boulder, and any noise might mean disaster. So he moved slowly and quietly, taking each step carefully in the darkness. He stopped several times to listen to the night for any noises that seemed out of place, anything that might make him worry that the Stallings brothers and their men were attempting to sneak up on the lieutenant. Surely, Stout believed, they would attempt to get at the lieutenant's position under the cover of night.

So he waited, hidden by the darkness, near the base of the cliff where the lieutenant had hunkered down. He leaned his rifle against the rock face where it would be easy to find in the dark, though he did not intend to fire the rifle.

They would not come in great numbers, Stout decided. They would not risk all of their men. Maybe five or six. Stout's one advantage was that he knew anybody he encountered in the darkness would be an enemy. His thoughts drifted between Faustina, at home in the cabin in San Luis, the sergeant, riding alone and injured down a dark trail, and the lieutenant, perched on the ledge not far away, no idea that the scout who had guided him into these mountains was now just a few feet away.

Faustina would have a fire going in the stove and would be under a blanket. By now she was probably in bed, probably asleep. She might be lying awake, wondering about her husband. Her guess would be that he was riding dispatches to Santa Fe, though often when he rode south from the fort he would stop and spend the night at their cabin, and he'd not done so this trip. Even so, likely she would not have much concern for danger beyond the worries any wife had when her husband traveled in this rough country.

The sergeant would push himself and the horses, and that could be a problem. A rock or a hole might be enough to break a horse's leg, send the sergeant tumbling. Stout winced at the thought. Thrown from the horse, maybe with a broken leg or a bashed head, the sergeant would die alone on the trail, and their one hope for salvation, a posse from Del Norte, might never come if the sergeant was overly vigorous in his nighttime ride.

He resisted the urge to announce himself to the lieutenant, though the idea crossed his mind. But if anyone was approaching and heard, Stout's plan to help defend the lieutenant's position would be exposed.

These thoughts alternated in Stout's mind over the hours of darkness, but his head cleared instantly when he heard faint whispers in the darkness.

His body went taut as wrapped his fingers around the grip of the knife on his belt, and he strained his ears for any sound that might confirm what he thought he'd heard.

At first there was nothing, but then he heard a muffled grunt – a man who'd just stubbed his toe against a root or cracked his knee against a boulder. The grunt was followed by a soft whisper, perhaps a word of warning to other men to avoid the same obstacle.

Stout guessed they were probably only about twenty feet or so below him on the hillside.

The scout squinted into the darkness. He wanted to see a dark shape move to give him his bearings, give him some idea of what he was up against. But even if he didn't see a shadow against the night, this was it. The moment he'd come here for. The Stallings outfit was making its approach against the lieutenant – maybe just a couple of men, maybe the entire body.

Had the lieutenant heard? Was he alert to the threat?

The absence of any moonlight made everything almost pitch black, but the stars shone in the clear night, and Stout knew that there would be light enough to see when the men were close enough. He pressed himself against the wall of the cliff, making ready to grapple with the first shape he saw.

Levi Stout was a strong man, and he didn't hardly know fear in a fist fight or a knife fight. He believed there weren't any two men on this earth that he couldn't take in a fight, and it would be a rough crew of three who could take him. In the dark like this, knowing himself and knowing how ferocious he could be, Stout would give himself odds against five men.

"Come on," he said soundlessly to himself, urging forward the men on the hillside. "Get up here. Let's get this part over with."

And then he saw the first shape, so near that Stout could almost reach out and touch him. And then another shape, and another. He could hear them now, too, their boots scratching against the ground as they moved gingerly to avoid walking into a boulder or a fallen tree. Maybe there were five or six men out there, but he didn't think more than that.

Stout made no noise. He just stood, poised and ready.

"One more step," he thought to himself.

His left hand shot out and grabbed the shirt front of the shape in front of him, his right hand swept the knife from its scabbard, twisting it so that the cutting blade pointed toward the sky, and he swung the blade up in an arc that ripped into the shape's stomach.

The man shouted – both from surprise and the sudden pain. Stout did not let go of the shirt front, his own arm acting as a guide for the point at which he wanted to bury the knife. He reared back with the knife and jabbed it straight forward with enough force to plant the knife deep in the shape's upper chest, maybe even right at the base of the throat.

The shout died away as Stout turned loose of the shirt

front and let the man stumble back.

Now he leapt forward toward the next shape, jabbing with his fist and the knife all at once. He felt pain shoot through his knuckles as his fist collided hard with a jaw, and that man also fell away.

"Hey!" a voice shouted, and Stout swung the knife wildly at the sound of the voice. He missed, but took a step forward and swung again, and this time the knife cut into flesh. The voice shouted again, a guttural response to being cut.

Stout sensed that he'd made his way in among them now, and there was confusion. The cavalry scout began throwing wild punches. When he made contact with a shoulder or face or chest, he closed and fought viciously with anything that he could grab hold to. Someone swung a rifle that collided with Stout's arm, but the scout grabbed the rifle and jerked it loose from the man who'd swung it. The man tripped and fell into Stout's leg. Now the scout dropped toward the ground, bringing the knife down, and he stabbed the fallen man in the back.

The commotion, of course, roused the lieutenant, who now fired a shot into the darkness from the ledge above.

"Hold your fire!" Stout yelled, not sure if the lieutenant would or not.

Stout reached out into the darkness and his hand caught hold of a pant leg. He gave an almighty jerk and dropped the man to the ground. The man tried to roll away, but Stout had a firm grip, and he scrambled up on top of the man and brought down the knife in brutal fashion.

Around him, men were grunting in pain and confusion. Lieutenant Turner fired another shot into the mass below him, but if either of the shots struck a target, Stout didn't know. From the trees farther down the trail a volley erupted. Several shots all fired within a couple of seconds. They were shooting at the muzzle flash, but Stout did not think they would fire again. They were risking their own men shooting into the darkness.

Blindly, Stout reached for another target but found nothing. He got to his feet in a crouch, swinging the knife and grabbing at the darkness.

He heard a man running – scrambling back down the hillside – and the man fell and grunted and shouted as he went head first down the slope. Again, Stout swung wildly with the knife, trying to find a target. He punched at the darkness and then twisted round and jabbed the knife, but as fast as the violence erupted it had died away. There were no targets around him. Anyone left alive had retreated back down the hillside.

The rifle on the ledge above barked again and then another time, and Stout sensed that the shots were getting close to him.

"Lieutenant Turner!" Stout shouted. "Stop shooting."

- 17 -

"Mr. Stout?" Turner's voice called back from the ledge. "Is that you?"

"It is me, but it won't be much longer if you fire that rifle again."

"What?" the lieutenant asked, but he could not be more articulate than that.

"I come back to lend a hand," Stout said. "Now hold your fire. I'm coming up to join you."

Stout made his way slowly back to the cliff face and found his rifle and possibles bag. From there, he had to fumble his way in the dark to try to climb to Turner's ledge.

"What's happened down there?" Turner asked as Stout attempted to find a way up. "Where's Sergeant O'Keefe? And why have you come back?"

"Hang on," Stout said, his breathing heavy as he struggled to find a handhold on the rock. "Can you take my rifle?"

Stout tapped it against the rock and in a moment, Turner found it and pulled it up. Now the scout followed and then he was up on the ledge and inside the lieutenant's fortification. Turner gave Stout just a moment to catch his breath before again peppering him with questions.

"What are you doing here, Mr. Stout? Where is Sergeant O'Keefe?"

Stout spoke in a hushed voice. He did not know if any men might still be in earshot. "Could I suggest, Lieutenant, that you keep your voice down. Those men might still be nearby, and it would be too easy for them to get past this position in the dark and pursue Sergeant O'Keefe. Like I said, Lieutenant, I turned back to help you. Sergeant O'Keefe has continued on to Del Norte."

"Alone?" Turner asked.

Stout grunted.

"I decided you stood a better chance of holding these men off with me here to help, and Sergeant O'Keefe can manage to get himself back to Del Norte."

Turner started to give voice to his anger, but he stopped himself. He took a calming breath before he spoke, and he kept his voice to a whisper.

"Mr. Stout, I told you to go on to Del Norte," Turner

said. "This is a delaying action and nothing more. There's small chance of making it out of this alive. My intention was to delay these men to give you and Mr. O'Keefe time to get to Del Norte so that we can ensure these men are brought to justice."

"I'm here now, and it is what it is," Stout said. "But we need to move out of this place by dawn."

"Move out?" Turner said. "I chose this place because it is an ideal ground from which to cover the trail below. Those men can't get at me here."

"Those men almost got at you here," Stout said. "If I hadn't been down there, they'd have had you just now. And they'll get the both of us if we stay here. It's time to get moving."

Turner's voice rose now, his anger compounded. The scout had disobeyed him by coming back, and now was arguing that they should abandon what Turner believed to be an ideal position.

"I don't intend to move, Mr. Stout."

"We can do better than just giving up our lives, Lieutenant," Stout said. "And if we stay here, that's what we'll do. Sooner or later, they'll figure out a way to get at us. They've got enough men to make it happen."

Turner sat quietly for a moment. He knew it was true what the scout said. If Stout hadn't been down below to greet those men in the dark, they'd have likely gotten to the lieutenant, and he realized it. He also knew that he'd turned back and committed himself to this delaying action because this was the way he could avoid humiliation – either through a successful action, as unlikely as that was, or by sacrificing his own life. Begrudgingly, the lieutenant had to admit to himself that he'd turned back and climbed to this ledge to die rather than face a trial for his failure of leadership.

"What do you propose?" the lieutenant asked.

Stout breathed a sigh of relief. He'd worked for plenty of young officers, men more worried about how their actions would be perceived by their superior officers than they were about their own lives. He understood the man, even if he did not know the man. And Levi Stout knew as well as Elliot Turner what impulse drove the young lieutenant back to this place. If he could convince the lieutenant there was a better way, Stout might yet be able to get them both out of this alive.

"Our purpose is to delay these men," Stout said. "So let's delay them. They cannot let us live. Their future depends on killing us in these mountains and making it appear that we were killed by Indians. If dawn breaks and we're not here, they'll have to come after us, and if we can keep ahead of them, we can give Sergeant O'Keefe the time he needs to get to Del Norte."

"You're determined that we abandon this position?" Lieutenant Turner said.

"We can last longer on foot than we can holed up here," Stout said.

"All right then," Turner agreed. "I'll defer to your judgment, Mr. Stout."

- 18 -

"There's not but three of them up there," Lou Stallings growled. "We know how many there were, we know how many we killed back at the camp, and we know how many are still alive. It's not more than three."

Dicky Cort shrugged his shoulders and looked at the flames of the campfire. They'd built it down below a hill and behind enough cedars that the men on the ledge wouldn't be able to see it glowing, and most of Stallings' outfit was huddled near the fire.

"Well, they fought like five or six men," Dicky said. He held out the front of his coat and showed where the knife had slice it. "I'm lucky to be alive."

Stallings had sent five men, led by Dicky Cort, to make their way in the darkness to the ledge. As best as he could tell from the fighting during the day, only one man was up there. Dicky and the others got to the base of the rock cliff, and according to him they were jumped in the dark by at least four men, and Dicky thought it was more like five or six.

It was true, in the firelight the four men who returned looked like they'd been beaten on by a group of men. Dicky's cut coat was the least of his troubles. His nose was broken, and maybe a couple of ribs. One of the other men had a bad stab wound, and some of the others were trying to get that to stop bleeding. And one of the men had a broken jaw. And they'd lost one man. He never came back. Whether he was dead, incapacitated, or disappeared just like Tommy Irons, Lou Stallings didn't know. At this point, Lou didn't much care. They'd had a simple plan, and somehow it had all come undone. The soldiers arrived much faster than anyone expected. In truth, Lou half thought the soldiers wouldn't come at all, this close to winter.

"What are we going to do?" Jacob hissed at his older brother. "Everything has gone to hell."

"We'll take care of it," Lou said. "It's not but three men."

Their first claim on the eastern range, the first one they ever sold, had been done like this. But it was just Lou and Jacob and Phil Wells then. Two prospectors struck gold. They came down into the camp where the Stallings brothers and Wells were drinking in a tent saloon, bemoaning their lack of luck. These two prospectors drank it up pretty good that night and boasted of their strike. Come morning, when the prospectors made their way back to their claim, Lou and Phil followed them. It was

Jacob's idea, but it was Lou and Phil who followed them. They dropped the bodies of those two prospectors down in a gulch, and then Jacob filed the claim. It was that easy. Nobody asked about those two prospectors. Nobody questioned whether the Stallings brothers owned the claim or had rights to sell it. Nobody suspected a thing.

They sold that claim and they made other finds that they sold, too. Jacob began to build a reputation for himself as a man who could sniff out gold. But in truth, all the big claims, all the ones that prospered, had started as someone else's claim. What Jacob could sniff out was prospectors who'd just struck a big one. And that was the important part – catching these men before they had an opportunity to file. That's what prevented questions from being asked.

Jacob inched closer to the fire. He hated the cold. He hated the mountains. And in his depressed mood, he was beginning to feel the noose tightening around his neck. They'd hang for sure for what they'd done.

"You said it wasn't but the one up there," Jacob said. "Now it's all three of them."

"Obviously, they were waiting for us," Lou said. "It was a ruse, just the one up on the ledge. The other two must've been hiding, waiting. Tommy Irons said he knows one of the men."

"What the hell happened to Tommy?" Jacob asked. They'd not seen him again all day, and that had Lou worried, too. He didn't think anything had happened to Tommy, but if there was a man who'd left the outfit, that could be dangerous to all of them. One thing at a time, though. The soldiers were the most pressing concern.

"I don't know," Lou said. "We'll worry about Tommy Irons later. Best thing to do now is bed down. We'll leave a couple of men to keep watch, and before dawn we'll move to surround that position up on the hill. Come morning, we'll rush those soldiers and finish this off."

DAY TWO

- 19 -

Even in the dark before dawn, it did not take long for Levi Stout to work his way back to the horse.

He had a sixth sense for moving across rough terrain. Where other men in the pitch dark would stumble on rocks or over branches or lose their footing on a slope, Levi Stout's feet seemed to always find the right place to light. Stout felt around with his toes down at the base of the cliff, and he found only one body there. He thought he'd probably killed two or three men, but it seemed the others made it off the hillside. Maybe they didn't make it all the way down, or maybe they had mortal wounds when they got back to camp. The scout almost felt sorry he'd not done a more thorough job in the fight, not that he was keen to take a life, but the more of them he took the fewer there would be to try him again later.

The two cavalry men moved silently, worried that those men in the woods below them might have come out under the cover of darkness and set up for a dawn attack. Indeed, at one point, Stout was certain he heard from not far away the sound of metal tapping wood, perhaps a belt buckle against the stock of a gun.

Stout had slept little during the night on the ledge, only dozing for a short while before relieving the lieutenant by keeping watch. And then, before the first light of dawn, the two men slipped down from the ledge and made their way down to where Stout had left the horse.

"We've got to make them believe there are three of us, still," Stout said. "They didn't attack our camp by chance – they'd seen us and knew our numbers. So they know there are three of us who escaped the attack."

"How do we make them think there are three of us?" Turner asked.

"You and I walk. On purpose, we find mud and snow to leave our tracks. We lead the horse. With luck, they'll think there's a third man on the horse. They probably know one of us is injured, so they'll think the injured man is riding. And then we just stay ahead of them. They'll follow us. And that should give O'Keefe time to get to Del Norte."

And so the two men walked, leading the horse. After dawn, but still in the early morning, they came upon a trail leading back north into the higher elevations, they left the trail to Del Norte, following a lesser traveled path taken by prospectors, and probably Ute hunting parties before them. As they took the new path, Stout walked the horse in circles, planted his own feet in mud, and even purposefully slid a foot down the new path to leave a clear and obvious mark.

"No point in leading them up the wrong trail if they don't take the bait," Stout muttered in explanation.

"Will they not suspect something when they see we've left the trail for Del Norte?" Lieutenant Turner asked. "The only reasonable course of action for us is to go to Del Norte."

Stout shrugged, tugging the reins to get the horse moving up the new path.

"Let 'em suspect," he said. "It doesn't matter what they think. All that matters is that they follow us up this trail. And they will follow. They can't jump a claim if they're hanging from the end of a rope."

The two men walked on through the high hills, following a path that skirted the edge of an evergreen forest. The trail alternated between slight increases in elevation, at times almost imperceptible, and steeper grades that left their thighs aching and both men breathing hard.

At nearly every creek, no matter how narrow or shallow, they found abandoned shelters. Some were not much more than lean-tos, something to keep the rain off, while others were log cabins but without much in the way of chinking or even very much skinning of the trees to try to set the logs level. They gapped such that any wind that wanted to blow inside was free to do so, but most of them had roofs that didn't leak too bad.

"Summer lodgings," Stout said without any admiration. "They didn't spend much time on them because they knew they'd abandon them come winter. They just needed a place to sleep at night where they could feel safe from the bears and cougars and such."

They kept a steady pace and resisted the urge to take turns riding, even as the patches of snow became more common until at last they reached a height where the trail became covered in snow. And there they began to trudge, their progress slower as the cold and the higher elevation began to work against them.

It was here, with an uninterrupted view of the mountains to their west and the evergreens reaching high above them to the east that Stout began to worry.

"Dark sky off that way," he noted with a nod to the left.

Turner examined the clouds, gray and low and rolling.

"More snow?" he asked.

"Looks to be," Stout grumbled. "We may have done our job too well."

"How so?" Turner asked.

"If it's a big snow, those men following us could be days stuck up in these mountains. But we'd be in just as bad a shape. Of course, I reckon it's possible the snow could bury our tracks and give us a chance to double back, get in behind them. If we could manage it without being seen, we could make for Del Norte."

As the clouds moved closer and covered the afternoon sun, the men continued to climb, they reached a great bald patch of the mountain where the rocky cliff rose to a peak above them and they could climb no higher. Here they followed the trail along a long, barren saddle still covered in large patches of icy snow, and the wind blew so hard that they had to press their hats down to keep them. Turner noted out loud the distinct drop in temperature, but he had to repeat himself for Stout to hear him over the wind.

"We'll need to get down to the trees and make camp," Stout said back. "It's going to be a bitter night. With a little luck, that party following us will find themselves huddled down here when night falls."

"Do you think they're still following us?" Turner asked.

"If we're still alive, they're still following us," Stout said.

They continued out across the alpine tundra, and now the snow began to fall. It was light at first, just a little, and with the clouds getting caught on the distant peaks and blowing like smoke from a fire, it made for quite a sight that Turner had never seen, and hoped he would never see again. He did not like the mountains. He was cold under his clothes, cold in his flesh and down in his bones, and he knew the cold he felt now was nothing to what the night would bring. And he worried about the coming night. How could they hope to survive it?

At last, though, as the trail cut across the tundra's dips and climbs, they reached a point where a small forest of spruce trees grew tight together.

"There?" Turner called ahead to Stout.

The scout had advanced several yards ahead of Turner now as the young lieutenant found it increasingly difficult to keep up with the man.

Stout turned. "How's that?" he asked.

"That copse of evergreens," Turner said, nodding his

head. "Should we make camp there?"

"Not there," Stout said. "We could find shelter there, but it's too early yet. They'll have us before dark if we stop there."

Stout turned ahead and kept walking. Turner shook his head. He felt exhausted. The cold air hurt his teeth, his throat, his lungs, and yet he could not help but take heaping breaths of it. His muscles were sore, and he could not imagine how much worse his legs would be come morning. He was hungry. They'd not stopped all day to eat. They'd breakfasted only on the miles they consumed. Though Stout several times made Turner take drinks from his canteen, even when he protested that he was not thirsty.

He had a grudging admiration for the scout. Levi Stout was probably ten, maybe fifteen years his elder, but the man moved along the trail with an easy carelessness. Turner wondered at how a man became so hardy, so toughened against arduous travel, so indifferent to mortal danger. He'd not heard Stout even once grumble against the conditions or the circumstances. The cavalrymen, good Lord how they grumbled. But not Stout. Nor did he pause with indecision – this man was all decisive action.

Turner envied the man. He did not concern himself with the adornments of glory nor with fear of failure. He simply judged what best to do and went about it.

The snow continued to fall. Stout continued to trudge ahead, leading the horse. At last, Lieutenant Turner caught his breath sufficient and started behind him.

- 20 -

Lou Stallings did not like the thought of again dividing his outfit, but there was no choice in it. They had wounded men now, and another dead one at the base of the rock cliff.

When dawn broke, Lou and a half dozen men were poised down in a cluster of cedars at the base of the hillside. Quietly, with the first light, they made their way up to the cliff face just below the ledge where they knew the cavalryman had been the day before. After some time of no activity up on the ledge, Lou threw a rock up there. There was no response, so he sent one of his men to have a look. They all kept their rifles trained on the ledge as the man climbed up. But the ledge was empty.

"They've snuck out on us," Lou declared.

And then he concluded he would have to divide the men.

Out of pure orneriness, Lou decided Jacob should join those going in pursuit. This wasn't the sort of duty that came easily or naturally to his younger brother, but it was Jacob who'd gotten them into all this, and Lou was going to make damned sure that Jacob would get his share of whatever more trouble lay ahead. He brought along Dicky Cort, too, but with Phil Wells dead and Tommy Irons still missing, Lou was fast running out of men he could trust to tote water. Dicky was the last really good man in the bunch.

He sent four men with the three wounded and told them to take the horses and mules and bury the bodies of the men killed.

"Get it done where they won't be found," Lou said. "The last thing we need now is for some band of prospectors to come along and find all these dead soldiers and you men burying our dead. Get it done fast, and then hold up at Willow Creek. It may be a day or two, but you wait for us there."

With Jacob and himself included, Lou set off an hour or so after dawn with nine mounted men in pursuit of two cavalrymen and one scout who Tommy Irons said was a solid man.

Lou Stallings was no tracker, not like Tommy Irons, but he could find a foot print as well as the next man. He picked up the trail pretty fast, and only a couple of times did he have to dismount and really look hard to be sure they were still on the trail.

"They ain't bashful about where they're going," Lou said. "Two of them are on foot. They've got the wounded man riding. But that means they ain't going fast. We'll catch them by noon."

But then they came to the path that turned north and went higher into the mountains, and there Lou and all the others dismounted.

"Everything makes it look like they went up this away," Lou said.

"But this here is the trail to Del Norte," Jacob said. "Why would they cut to the north?"

Lou pointed out the tracks. They were obvious, even to Jacob who could only read a trail if someone else pointed it out to him, and Jacob couldn't argue what the signs looked like. But he could argue against the wisdom of the cavalrymen going north. It made no sense to him. All that made sense was that they would make for Del Norte as fast as they could go.

"Tommy Irons says that scout knows his business," Lou said. "Maybe he knows something we don't know. Maybe there's another trail to Del Norte. But we ain't catching them settin' here talking about it."

So the men gave up the debate and headed north on a trail that would take them higher, past the cold streams where men toiled for dreams through the summer and early autumn. They passed by the abandoned cabins and lean-tos, and the evidence of the summer's occupations left scattered by the huts and the streams – broken wheelbarrows, busted cradles, empty cans, even worn-through boots and shirts, cold fire pits. In a few months, when the snow began to melt, the men would return, most of them with pans and cradles who would seek and find nothing more than placer gold, enough to buy lodgings come the next winter. The life of a prospector was a terrible cycle of hope and disappointment, but the thrill of the dream would bring them back year after year until pneumonia or a knife in a saloon brought them their final reward.

Lou Stallings ignored it all. He didn't have the imagination to care about the lives of other men or the remnants of their dreams discarded along his route. He kept his eyes on the trail, looking for the signs that he continued on the right path. And he found the signs were plentiful. The tracks in the mud – even in easily avoided patches of snow – showed that he continued on the right track, though he remained perplexed as to why those soldiers would have come this way.

They kept their horses at a walk. Maybe if they'd stirred them to a lope, the Stallings outfit would have caught up to the three cavalrymen they sought, but Lou Stallings worried that if they went faster than a walk, they would lose the trail, miss some turn, and he wasn't sure that he was a good enough tracker to ever pick up the trail again. So they walked, staying assured that they were still trailing the men they were after. Even at a walk, Lou knew his mounted party must catch the cavalrymen who were afoot – if not by dusk than surely in the morning. All that mattered was that they followed the right trail.

By mid-afternoon, Jacob Stallings began to grow uneasy.

He did not consider himself much of an outdoorsman, but he'd spent enough time in the mountains seeking gold that he knew a thing or two. For instance, he knew that they'd climbed too high. The temperature began to drop. The wind picked up. They were leaving behind the cover of the evergreens where they could easily find shelter for making a camp. They were coming up to the high hills, the tundra where they'd struggle to find fuel for a fire, where the wind would get at them. They'd left their tents below with the pack mules and the wounded men. All they had to keep them warm were blankets. Down among the spruce, they could cut branches to build makeshift shelters and good windbreaks, and they could build up fires that would beat back the cold. But here, they'd have no makeshift shelters, and the brush available to them wouldn't make much of a fire. If they got stuck up this high at dark, they'd be forced to shelter against a cold granite wall in the hopes that it would block some of the wind, and their blankets would be poor substitute for a decent bedroll and the canvas walls of a tent protected by tall evergreens.

And then the clouds rolled in and the snow began, and when he looked back, Jacob Stallings could not even see how far they'd come from the tree line, and when he looked forward, Jacob could not see anything but more of the same. Granite peaks. Barren hills covered in snow.

"This is no place to be caught at dark," he said to his brother.

But Lou only had an interest in the tracks in the snow. Two men afoot and one horse.

"We can't stop now," Lou said. "We've got their trail."

So the nine men rode on, but Jacob Stallings was not the only man in the company who was having second thoughts about this expedition. He just couldn't figure out a way to get out of it now.

- 21 -

Tommy Irons spent a cold night beside a fire he'd made up against a sandstone cliff. The cliff blocked the wind, but Tommy had no blanket and only his coat to keep him warm. His mind was made up, he'd not be staying on with Lou Stallings and this outfit. Already they'd done too much. Tommy Irons didn't flinch at killing another man, even killing him to rob him. But they'd killed a patrol of soldiers, now, and whether Lou or Jacob or any of the others knew it, they had signed their death warrants. Killing a few prospectors, making it look like Indians had done it – that was a thing that could be done without retribution. But killing a patrol of soldiers, that was too much.

Before first light, Tommy Irons stomped out his fire and started down to the forest.

He made his way slowly in the dark, working his way among the pines and firs, careful of where he stepped. Tommy Irons always did have good eyesight. He could see farther than most, he could spot tracks and signs along a trail that others would miss, and he had a knack for finding his way in the pitch dark. Tommy had no fear of getting lost. He did not even need to lean on his innate sense of direction. The smell of smoke led him close to where the other men in his outfit had made camp.

As Tommy came upon them, he saw men stirring. They were clearly making some plans, and when he remembered the shots he'd heard in the middle of the night, he assumed the men had the cavalrymen cornered. But Tommy Irons knew, too, that one of those cavalrymen was Levi Stout, and Tommy knew that Stout would be like a cornered bear. Tommy wanted no part of this fight.

So he skirted the camp made by the other men in Stallings' outfit, silently crossing out of the reach of the light, avoiding being seen or heard. They'd built up the fire and made camp some distance from where the soldiers had camped with a wall of cedars completely blocking one campsite from the other. Tommy made his way now to where the soldiers had been camped, the place where the slaughter had occurred almost twenty-four hours prior. By the time he worked his way here, a gray light was showing beyond the canopy of the trees, and Tommy Irons found himself crawling through the low branches of first to get what he needed.

The soldiers' saddles were stacked near to the trees. Tommy found all that he needed, blanket and saddle, bridle and rope, and even saddlebags. He saw rifles leaning against a tree out in the open, but decided not to chance it. He knew the soldiers' horses would be down in the valley below, and he intended to ride out of here as fast as possible. He would pass by Del Norte by a wide margin and make for one of the little villages farther to the south. Then maybe he'd try to beat winter to Santa Fe. He had friends in Santa Fe and could start over down there, away from Colorado Territory, away from Levi Stout, and away from Jacob and Lou Stallings.

He might even change his name again. It would not be the first time.

Dawn broke before Tommy had a horse, but not long after the first rays of daylight hit the valley, Tommy Irons was riding out on the road to Del Norte.

On a cavalry horse wearing the U.S. brand and riding with a cavalryman's saddle, Tommy had no interest in seeing another person. But he also wanted to get as far away as possible. So he veered from the road at the first opportunity, riding out across the river and following along on the flat spaces there.

By noon, Tommy Irons was sure he'd left behind him whatever troubles Jacob and Lou Stallings were creating for themselves and those men who stayed with their group.

- 22 -

Sergeant Patrick O'Keefe turned twenty-eight years old on his most recent birthday. Born in Sligo, he'd emigrated to "Americay" when he was still just a boy. They settled in New York where they lived among the other Irish, and O'Keefe never could see that one place was much different from the other, nor much better. They said there was opportunity in America, but young Paddy's father worked at the docks and his mother washed other people's clothes, and he didn't see them working any less or earning any more. Still, his father being Irish, he was forever hopeful.

When the war broke out, he was just thirteen or

fourteen years old, and the notion of joining up with the United States army was hotly debated among his people.

Paddy's own father didn't wait for the draft. An independent minded man, he agreed with many of his neighbors that he feared the cheap black labor of free slaves, but he also opposed slavery. So he signed on with a Fenian brigade at the outbreak of war. To help the family, Paddy took a job driving freight from the docks through the city. He despised the work. He got caught up in the riots of '63, not so much because he had a political notion but because his friends followed their fathers into the rioting and Paddy was swept away with them. He was there when they burned the Bull's Head, and when he returned home some days later, beaten and hungry and exhausted, his own mother went into a rampage.

"Yer da is away fighting and you join up with the mob," she accused. The words that followed were vicious, the accusations incendiary, and Paddy O'Keefe found himself well-cowed.

Ashamed, Paddy enlisted the next day.

When the war ended, the elder O'Keefe returned home, but the younger O'Keefe, who'd seen action and given a good account of himself, said he'd stay on to fight the Indians. He went west and had never yet returned to New York. Through letters, he'd reconciled with his ma, and he'd thought many times when he had leave from the army that maybe he'd take the train to go back to see them. He desperately wanted to.

And now, he figured, he'd have the chance. He could return home, a maimed veteran who'd survived the war and the Indians only to be brought down by some damned claim jumpers.

He did not think a doctor would be able to save his

leg.

Ever since Stout had left him, he'd been in intense pain. Even riding the horse at a walk was terribly uncomfortable, and several times after Stout left him alone the day before, he'd had to halt the horse and climb out of the saddle and sit for a spell. Of course, climbing back into the saddle caused enough new pain that he immediately regretted each stop. But he also switched out horses each time he stopped, keeping the horses fresh. So when night fell, Sergeant O'Keefe continued to ride. He felt frozen in the saddle. The chill of the night air left the cavalryman frozen in the saddle, and well after dark he finally rounded up the horses, led them into a grassy patch off the trail and dropped himself down off the horse.

He managed to get the horses all picketed, but the effort of it was all he could stand. As much as he would have liked to scout out some firewood and make up a fire to keep him warm through the night, O'Keefe had done all he could manage. He kept his heavy coat on and his boots, and he covered himself with a blanket.

O'Keefe slept only in fits and starts through the night. Bitterly cold, and hungry, O'Keefe realized at some point during the night that the pain in his leg had subsided and now the thing was simply numb. He took that as a bad sign, and it was then that he began to believe he would not keep the leg.

A howling coyote somewhere nearby woke him just as he'd started to doze again. He imagined himself returning home to New York, one leg gone to a doctor's saw, and the life he saw ahead of him seemed worthless. He'd be nothing more than a pauper now. Probably he would rely on his parents if he wasn't too much of a burden to them, or maybe it would be the soldiers' home for him.

He intended to rise before dawn and get moving, but the cold was such that he could not force himself out from under the blanket.

So at dawn, O'Keefe finally rose from his earthen bed and saddled one of the horses. He tied up his blanket and then started the horses forward to Del Norte. He trotted a ways until he could no longer stand it. His leg was not causing him pain, but the numbness created a discomfort that made him wish the thing was already gone. If he thought he could do it, he'd cut the thing off himself. The cold air worked its way into his torn pants. O'Keefe imagined that the wound was already black with frostbite. Why else would it have turned numb? In truth, he was scared to see it unwrapped from his bandages and scared to get to a doctor and scared, at the same time, not to get to a doctor.

When Stout left him on his own, O'Keefe read in the scout's actions a confidence that he would survive, but now he began to even worry about that. Two men had gone back with a willingness to sacrifice their own lives so that O'Keefe could get to Del Norte, but now he wasn't sure he would make it. The lack of sleep, the hunger, the cold, the pain and discomfort, and the fear all combined inside the man to weaken his resolve.

But the sun brought a touch of warmth to the river valley, and the music of the Rio Grande flowing over its rocky course near the trail cheered him a bit. Being Irish, he was fond of music in any way he could find it, and he heard the music of the river in a way that other men did not.

As the sun warmed him, O'Keefe began to sing barely-decent songs of bawdy women to the horses, songs he'd sung as a boy out of the earshot of his ma, and the tunes cheered him a bit.

Around mid-morning, he changed horses once, and he found that it hurt his leg to put any weight on it. O'Keefe took the pain as a better sign than the numbness, and as he rode along on the fresh mount, he began to think that maybe his lot wasn't so bad after all. His dark mood lifted some.

He wondered how the young lieutenant and the scout were faring. Were they still holding off those men? He said the names to himself: Lou Stallings and Jacob Stallings and Tommy Irons. Those were the names he had to give them in Del Norte.

At best he would make Del Norte late tomorrow afternoon, and that was if he managed to keep riding through the night. He mostly only walked the horses, though a few times he got them up to a trot for a short distance. Up and down hills, out across grassy knolls, skirting forests of pine and cedar or clusters of aspen. He did his best to stay clear of the forests, though. The trail was worn enough that he didn't have to worry much, but in the forest his mount might step in a hole or trip over a fallen tree, and O'Keefe worried that a spill from the saddle might be all he could take.

He ate some of the jerky in the saddlebag and drank from his canteen, and late in the day as the sun dropped below the western mountains and the light began to fade dramatically, O'Keefe rode the horses over to a spot near some deadfall. There he dismounted, grateful for the pain it caused to his leg. He picketed the horses and then gathered some wood. He built up a good fire, a fire that would help to keep him warm through the night. He camped right on the edge of a stand of trees, and those trees acted as a wind break. He did not try to build any shelter – the effort would have been too much. But the fire was warm and the blanket was warm, and O'Keefe thought that tonight he might get some sleep and maybe be more amenable to rising before dawn in the morning.

The sun disappeared and darkness descended around him, but the flames of his fire licked high and O'Keefe kept feeding logs to the fire. He felt warm and comfortable.

And then a noise caught his attention from the darkness out where the trail was. He looked at his horses and made certain none of them had gotten loose. He heard the noise again, and it was unmistakable – a horse was on the trail. He unsnapped the holster cover on his belt and touched the grip of his Smith and Wesson.

"Mind if I come up?" someone called from the darkness, and O'Keefe's heart skipped a beat.

"Who's there?" O'Keefe asked.

And then a man on foot leading a horse stepped into the ring of fire light, and O'Keefe strained his eyes to get a look at the man.

The man coughed a bit to clear his throat – a lonely rider who had not spoken all day. "Just a traveler heading to Del Norte. My name's Tommy Irons."

- 23 -

Lieutenant Turner wiped a gloved hand across his eyes to wipe away the windblown snow that had found its way under the brim of his cavalry hat.

He'd tied a yellow bandanna to protect his face, and it gave him a sense of warmth, of being snuggled in blankets. But his eyes now watered against the cold wind, and from the bridge of his nose to the brim of his hat, he felt frozen. If they followed any kind of trail, Turner could no longer discern it. His feet seemed to get constantly tangled in the brushy weeds that grew high up in the mountains. Stout spotted a mountain lake and veered from what Turner had thought was a trail they were on. A creek ran from the lake down a steep crevice. Neither the lake nor stream were yet frozen over, but that would not continue to be the case for many more days. Stout worked his way along a ridge until he found a slope that allowed them to follow the stream down lower. It dropped down a fifteen-foot drop and flowed through a small gully. Stout followed it until they came to the precipice of another ridge, and below they saw trees. The stream fell down a series a short drops that looked like the staircase for a very long-legged man, and it disappeared into the darkness of the spruce forest.

Turner found himself now constantly looking over his shoulder. It seemed impossible to him that their pursuers would not immediately be upon them. They'd walked through the day while those men chasing them were surely mounted, and it confounded him how they had not yet been caught.

But Stout seemed unperturbed at the notion. Turner never once caught Stout looking over his shoulder. He just kept steadily moving forward.

"They could be a hundred yards behind us, or two miles behind us," Stout said when the lieutenant asked him. "It don't hardly matter either way. We set out to lure them away to give the sergeant time to get to Del Norte. Every step we take furthers that end."

"What if they're not behind us at all?" Turner asked.

"They're behind us," Stout said confidently, though the man was beginning to grow concerned about that. Like Turner, he thought that by now that group with Tommy Irons should have caught up to them. But he'd calculated that there would have been delays. They wouldn't have moved before dawn, and they would have been slow to determine that Turner and Stout were no longer up on the cliff ledge. Maybe they had injured men to deal with.

Anything could have delayed them. But he and Turner and the horse had left a trail that was easily picked up and followed, and those men had Tommy Irons in their outfit.

They dropped down to the tree line, making a series of switchback turns so that the horse could manage the steeper parts of their trail, and there Stout followed along the edge of the trees until they reached the place where the stream entered the forest. Here he entered the tree line, following the stream. Now the snow that had blanketed the bare tundra was not so thick, much of it caught on branches of the tall spruce trees, and it made the going a little easier. Though both men already felt as if their feet were frozen. Their toes were numb, and Turner, particularly, unaccustomed to hiking through the mountains, was exhausted and sore.

"It'll be dark in an hour or so," Stout said. "My aim is to find a cabin or a lean-to or any sort of shelter. Come morning, we'll begin to double back. If we greet those men out in the open, it'll be a shooting match for as long as we can last. But if they get into these woods, we might be able to get around behind them, and then we'll start for Del Norte ourselves. I won't make you any promises, Lieutenant Turner, but there's a possibility we'll come out of this right."

Turner clenched his jaw. Getting out of this meant a court martial and disgrace.

"If it comes to a shooting match, you do what you can to get yourself clear and leave me to fend them off," Turner said.

"We'll see what happens when the times comes," Stout said.

A gray light filtered through the forest, the last of dusk diffused by the trees ushering in the darkness of night.

Stout breathed a sigh of relief when he saw ahead of them what he'd been seeking. There not far from the banks of the stream was a cradle, set up on high ground away from where the water would likely flood come spring, and tied to a sturdy tree. He'd suspected that if they followed the stream long enough, they would reach some sign that prospectors had been here. A cradle lashed to a tree was the best sign – it meant someone planned to come back, and that meant there was probably a cabin nearby.

The stream dropped down over a rocky shoal, probably twenty feet or more. It was the smallest of streams, but over the rocks it made a mighty roar. It would freeze up soon, and the evidence along the clear banks suggested that come the spring melt, the stream would grow considerably to sweep away any vegetation that thought about lighting here.

"Is that a cabin?" Turner asked, pointing to a dark place below them among the trees.

Stout squinted at it. They were not yet plunged in darkness, but it was dark enough that he could not yet make out the outline of a cabin. So he simply grunted a response. But when they got fifteen or twenty feet closer, he could see that indeed they'd come upon a cabin.

"Gather up whatever firewood you can find," Stout said. "Don't stray far. Darkness will be on us soon, and you won't find your way back."

Stout led the horse down to the cabin.

The men who built the cabin hadn't much worried about their accommodations. Clearly, the place was built to keep them dry from the summer rain storms, keep the safe from critters, and give them a place to bed down at night, and not much more. The cabin had a dirt floor. The logs were rough-hewn and notched quickly with just an ax so that they did not even pretend to fit tight. The men who built this cabin had not used a plane nor a level. No chinking was in place. The wind cut through the cabin's walls at will. But the roof was solid and would keep the snow off them, and in that moment, Levi Stout could not imagine a better place.

The cabin had probably housed five or six men and was plenty large enough for them.

He brought the horse into the cabin and tied a rope about chest height to keep the horse in the back half of the cabin. He quickly cut some cedar branches and shoved them into the widest gaps between the log walls, creating enough of a windbreak that in a few moments the place already felt a little better. Then Stout collected some wood. He built up a little fire in near the door. The door was nothing more than a few stout saplings shaved clean of bark and nailed to a couple of cross boards, and it leaked wind as bad as the rest of the place. In truth, the cabin had been built for two purposes, shelter from the rain and protection from bear, and it was only intended for summer use.

"If we intended to stay more than one night, I'd try to stuff these walls with cedar branches," Stout told Turner when the lieutenant arrived with an armful of wood. "As it is, we'll stay warm enough in here for one night."

The wind blew in through the gaps and carried most of the smoke off with it so that only a little smoke hung in the top of the rafters.

Stout made up a pot of coffee for the two of them, and they ate just enough of their jerky to back down some of the pangs they'd been feeling through the day.

"Do you think O'Keefe will make it?" Lieutenant Turner asked as he held his coffee in both hands.

Stout was setting his socks out on a rock by the fire.

"You should take off your boots, Lieutenant," he said. "Dry your socks. Take care of your feet. If we're getting out of here, we'll do it on our feet, so you've got to take care of them."

Turner nodded.

"That's good advice."

"O'Keefe had a good start and plenty of horses so that he's always got a fresh mount. If those men followed us, he'll get to Del Norte. Even if they gave up and turned back. If they figured out our ruse and stayed on the road to Del Norte, then he could be in trouble. They might have split their numbers, some of them after us and some after O'Keefe. It's hard to know for sure. But we've done what we could do."

"Maybe we should have stayed back on the ledge, tried to cover his retreat a while longer," Turner said.

"We did the right thing. We'd have been trapped up there and would have lasted only as long as our ammunition. Maybe an hour, maybe less. But if you're going to be a leader, it's my opinion that second thoughts are your enemy. Make a plan, follow the plan through to the end."

Turner slid his boots off and then pulled off his socks. His feet had gone numb and his toes stung against the sudden warmth from the fire.

"You're married, Stout?"

"I am," Stout said.

The lieutenant felt grateful for the bit of warmth from the fire. Darkness was now fully descended outside, and it seemed to him that anything outside the soft orange light of the fire must be unbearably cold.

"Where's your wife?" Turner asked.

"We've got a cabin in a little village south of Fort Garland," Stout said.

The scout had tried to force Faustina from his mind. He worried that if he focused too much on those parts of life beyond this trail, beyond this cabin, beyond this night, beyond those men following them, that he could become careless or ignore some important matter. He needed his mind focused on the present. He'd accepted when he left O'Keefe and came back that there might be no future.

"Do you have children?"

"None," Stout said, though the question made a dream flash through his mind.

Turner felt talkative and was undeterred by Stout's short responses.

"How long have you been an army scout?"

"I scouted for the cavalry during the Great Sioux Uprising in '62 and '63," Stout said. "Came west after that. I've been up in the Dakotas and all through the Sangre de Cristo Mountains. When I left the army, I worked for prospectors, guiding expeditions into the mountains. That's what I've done the last couple of years. That, and ride dispatches for the army."

"Do you like it?" Turner asked.

"Like what?"

"Being out of the army?"

Stout shrugged. "Most of the time it doesn't seem like I am. I ain't off on expeditions for months the way I used to be, but I still earn most of my wages from the army."

Stout broke a branch over his knee and put half of it into the fire.

"You'd best get some sleep, Lieutenant," he said. "Tomorrow's bound to be a rough day."

"We'll meet the enemy tomorrow?" Turner asked.

"We'll meet 'em, or we'll play hell getting away from them. Either way, you'll need all the sleep you can get. I'll take the first watch."

Turner bedded down beside the fire, and was grateful for the warmth of his blanket and fire. The previous night had been misery, freezing cold on that ledge.

He'd turned back to face the enemy with an idea that he would not survive it. He saw little value in living through this, considering the future that lay ahead of him. But now he considered that he might yet get from this some sort of decent outcome – if not glory, perhaps at least he could avoid humiliation at a court martial. If a posse could be got up in Del Norte, either by him and Stout or by Sergeant O'Keefe, then perhaps Turner could take charge of that posse and bring about some satisfactory conclusion. Any arrest of these men, or any battle that led to their deaths, where Turner took an active role in command, might yet redeem him in the eyes of his judges.

For his part, Levi Stout stayed awake, feeding the fire and thinking of his wife. He saw small chance that he and Turner would make it out of this alive. Tommy Irons was more than competent, and he would not be fooled again by tracks that doubled back. He'd be watching for it. Tommy would know there was nowhere this trail would take them that would lead to safety, and so he would be alert for them to try to turn on their pursuers. It would take a small miracle for them to get past Tommy Irons.

The snow would probably not be sufficient to hide their tracks, but if it continued to snow through the night, they might have a chance. Maybe, if Tommy was careless and Stout's luck held out, their pursuers were currently caught in the open up on the tundra – no shelter to protect them from the wind and snow. Maybe a cold night would be enough to convince those men to give up, or at least to leave them exhausted. There were still some factors that might yet provide Stout and the young lieutenant with the luck they needed.

- 24 -

Lou Stallings led his men through the saddle and out to a ridge surrounded by hills. The tracks were plain to see now, but the sun was setting and darkness would be upon them soon. The horses were stubborn in the cold, and Lou's horse balked at going farther. It was as if the horse sensed that it would be trapped and exposed if it continued on this path. The snow was beginning in earnest now, and whipped by the wind, horse and rider alike found it blinding.

"Ha!" Lou shouted at the horse and gave it a slap with the reins to keep it moving.

Jacob rode up even with his brother. He had tied a

scarf around his nose and mouth and ears and wrapped a blanket around his shoulders and was riding with just one gloved hand sticking out through a gap in the blanket. For the moment, he was settled in and warm enough.

"What do you think, Lou?" Jacob asked, casting a dubious eye at the tracks in the snow. "This ridge goes on for miles, and it'll be dark soon. We're going to get caught out."

"Do you want to catch them or not?" Lou Stallings asked.

"I don't want to freeze to death," Jacob said. He hated the cold and hated camping out, exposed to the elements. If they had a cabin, that would be one thing. He could stand it if they were in a cabin, at least. But there would be no cabins on this exposed ridge. The best they could do would be to hunker down against a cliff face and hope the wind didn't decide to shift overnight. They would find no fuel for a fire out here, no cedar boughs for a windbreak or shelter. All they would have to protect them from the cold would be their coats and their blankets.

Lou grunted a response, and Jacob did not know what he intended by it.

"I'm saying I don't think we should press on," Jacob said. In his prospecting expeditions, Jacob Stallings had hiked and ridden through countless mountain passes identical to this one, and he knew these tundra trails could go for miles up hills and down into hollows, and they could twist around cliffs in a way that a man could be hours trying to get back below to some sort of shelter. Once, in the summer, he'd seen a storm off in a distance and tried to get across a tundra pass before the storm hit. But he'd been unsuccessful, and found himself the tallest thing around, exposed to lightning and terrible wind and lashing rain. It had been a miserable experience, and Jacob spent the afternoon and night huddled at the base of a granite ledge, waiting out the storm. He feared they were headed into an identical situation, only it would be snow and freezing wind that would torment them this night.

"If we don't stop these men, they'll see us hanged in Del Norte or Denver or some damned place," Lou Stallings said. "By morning, the snow could cover their tracks. We've got them now, and we'd be damned fools to let them go. And you'll not turn back, neither. It was you who got us into this, and you'll stay with me until I've gotten us out."

And so they rode on, but Jacob Stallings did not like it. In truth, the snowfall was not so bad, but the wind seemed to increase the quantity and force of it. Jacob twisted in his saddle to get a look at the other men. Most had tied scarves around their faces, the same as he had. None objected out loud to pressing on. Like Lou said, these men were veterans, accustomed to doing as they were told. They were also hard men who didn't complain much about weather or much else besides their rate of pay.

Once Lou got his horse convinced that they were moving forward, the beast went on at a pretty good lope, and there was no need to rein him in. The tracks in the snow were plain to see, and they were on the right path. The gray clouds blotted out the sun entirely, but Jacob could guess that they had maybe an hour left of daylight.

They rode out over a white landscape, broken here and there by the granite cliffs so steep that the snow had not yet begun to cling to the sides. Distant peaks loomed like vast, gray pyramids floating in the sky as cloud and snow combined to erase from view the lower portion of the faraway mountains. Jacob Stallings reflected that it was a brutal beauty that could be found in these high places, a murderous beauty completely indifferent to the death it wrought.

Whatever came next, Jacob Stallings wanted no part of it, but he could not think of a way to extricate himself from it.

- 25 -

Sergeant O'Keefe eyed the silver blade of the knife, gleaming in the firelight. Under his blanket, his hand gripped the Smith and Wesson. He'd not give up easily, no matter how much pain he was in.

The half-breed Indian held the knife loosely in his hand, showing it to the army sergeant. He bore a gentle look as he nodded at the knife.

"I'm just going to cut those bandages off and take a look at the leg," Tommy Irons said.

"Go ahead," O'Keefe said.

Carefully, Tommy Irons slid the tip of the knife under

the bandages. They were stained and damp. He gripped one edge of the bandage and then slit the knife up, cutting away the bandage. O'Keefe held his breath. Even if the Indian did not intend to kill him, having the blade of that knife so near to his wound made him nervous.

Tommy twisted the leg slightly toward the fire, making O'Keefe wince and draw a sharp breath.

"It's a nasty gash, for sure," Tommy Irons said. He looked up into O'Keefe's face. "What'd you say you got into, Sergeant?"

"I didn't say," O'Keefe responded.

Tommy nodded his head.

They were playing a game, and both men knew it. Tommy Irons had adopted the narrative that he was a lonely prospector coming out of the mountains. He made no effort to explain the U.S. brand on his horse, nor the cavalry saddle. He pretended not to know about the slaughtered cavalrymen. O'Keefe played along. For his part, he pretended that Levi Stout had not said the name "Tommy Irons" to him, and he pretended not to notice the brand on the horse or to recognize the saddle.

O'Keefe was in a bad way right now. He couldn't hardly fight if it came to that, and if he missed with his first shot from the six-shooter, Tommy Irons would have him with his knife.

Tommy stood up and drew a flaming log from the fire. He held it out like a torch in front of him.

"Let it air out for a bit," he said. "Ignore the cold. I'm going to see what I can find that might help."

O'Keefe did not respond. He watched the man walk off into the darkness until the flame of the log disappeared.

The cold ached his leg, but he leaned back against his saddle and shut his eyes, trying not to think about his exposed leg.

Soon, though, exhaustion overcame him, and the sergeant began to doze behind his closed eyes.

A while later, O'Keefe couldn't say how much time had passed, the rattling of a tin woke him. Tommy Irons had returned and was bent over the fire. He'd added some branches to it and was boiling a tea.

Seeing the sergeant awake, Tommy took a tin cup in which he'd stirred some sort of paste, and he began to apply it to the wound.

"This should help to pull out the infection," he said. "You may save your leg, yet, Sergeant."

"I was asleep," O'Keefe said.

"For a while. I expect you needed some sleep."

He slathered the wound with the paste and then wrapped it in bandages he took from his own saddlebag. Like the horse, the saddlebag bore a U.S. marking.

"I'm going to ride into Del Norte," Tommy Irons said. "When I get there, I'm going to the livery. I know the man there, and he'll give me a fresh horse. Then I'm leaving out. I'll not be coming back to these parts. I'm done here."

As he spoke, Tommy Irons wrapped the leg. "Maybe go to Denver."

"Long ride to Denver," Sergeant O'Keefe said. "Hard ride this time of year, unless you go around the mountains."

"However I go, I'm done here," Tommy said. "If you want, I'll leave out in the morning before you. Or after, if you prefer. I'd rather go ahead of you."

Tommy tied of the bandage and then turned to the kettle on the fire. He poured a white-tinted liquid from the kettle into a cup.

"Let this cool for a moment, and then drink this. It will help with the pain."

O'Keefe took the cup and felt the warmth of it through his leather gloves. He held it close to his face but did not yet drink it. It smelled like cooked noodles with a bit of a woody smell, too, and when he took a sip of it, it tasted the same. It warmed him inside, and he did soon think that maybe he felt some relief from the pain in his leg.

Tommy Irons made up a bed on the straw over on the opposite side of the fire, and he put a couple of heavy logs in to keep the fire going for some time.

"I'll camp here and make certain you make it through the night," Tommy said. "You understand?"

"I understand," O'Keefe said. They were still playing their game, dancing around the edges of the truth that both of them knew.

And O'Keefe did understand. Whatever agreement Tommy Irons had with the Stallings brothers, the one-time army scout had decided to break the agreement. He wanted out and he intended to leave all that had happened behind him. He was caring for the sergeant as a sort of payment, to buy off his responsibility for his part in what had happened. O'Keefe was in no position to deny Tommy Irons what he wanted, but he also was in no position to grant it – not fully.

"I'll make a report in Del Norte," O'Keefe said. "I'll give them all the names I have."

Tommy Irons nodded his head.

"I'll leave out ahead of you in the morning."

DAY THREE

- 26 -

Lieutenant Turner woke to the scratch of a knife in a tin pot and the smell of bacon.

He opened his eyes and the cold of the air stung. In the smoky air of the cabin, he could smell bacon.

"Thought I'd heat us up some breakfast," Stout said. "We'll need our strength today."

A thick fog of smoke glowed in the orange light of the fire. Turner squinted through a gap in the log walls and saw that it was still pitch-black outside.

"What time is it?" he asked.

Stout grunted.

"Before sunup."

"You never woke me to keep watch," Turner said. "Did you not sleep?"

"I slept," Stout said. "I decided when it got late enough that there wasn't much chance they'd come at us in the dark. I figured you and I could both use a decent night's sleep."

Turner kept the blanket over him, unwilling yet to fully submit to the cold. His boots and socks were still on a rock near the fire. He'd taken off his coat to sleep and it was also near the fire.

"Soup's on," Stout said, sliding a crisp piece of bacon from the pan with his knife and lifting it up, balanced on the knife. He put thumb and forefinger to the bacon, and Turner could see that it was hot to touch. But the scout lifted the bacon from the knife and began eating it. "There's biscuits, too."

The biscuits were just a water and flour concoction cooked in the bacon grease and hardly deserving of the name, but Turner sat up, keeping the blanket wrapped around him, and took a piece of the bread from the hot pan. The two men ate in silence, and Turner began to wonder if Stout was preparing himself for the coming fight. Was this what it was like fighting Indians out on the plains? Did the men gather around a fire for a hot breakfast before sunup and gird themselves for battle? And the young lieutenant realized, too, that this was what he'd come for – to fight in the way that his father had fought, in the way that his uncle had fought. And he realized that what came next might be the only battle he would ever experience.

"Is this what it's always like?" Turner said.

The scout did not need to ask what he meant. He'd been in situations similar enough to this that he always understood the thoughts of the greenhorns. It was one of the reasons that Levi Stout preferred being a scout and being away from the troopers. When the greenhorns started to get nervous, it made everyone nervous.

"My plan, Lieutenant, is to locate these men following us, get a sense of their numbers, and then get in behind them. I don't want to get caught up in a firefight if we can help it. They've got us out-gunned. Even if they left half their number, they've got us out-gunned. So if we can avoid it, we shouldn't engage them in a shooting match."

Turner did not speak, and Stout looked up sharply at the man, narrowing his eyes.

"Of course, you're the officer. Maybe you've got a different plan in mind."

Turner chuckled and with a shrug of his shoulders turned his hands up.

"Mr. Stout, I don't have any idea what I would do differently," Turner said. "I'm following you."

The faintest morning light was showing in the sky above the canopy when Stout crushed out the coals of the fire and kicked dirt into the small fire pit.

"I'd hate for the men who built this place to turn up in spring and find it burned down," he said.

Stout took the lead rope of the horse, and the men stepped out of the cabin and into the cold forest. The snow had come down through the night, and Turner heard the crunch of snow under foot with most every step they took. They made no effort now to cover their tracks.

"If we're lucky, enough snow fell overnight to cover our tracks and they'll have lost us," Stout said. "If that happens, we've accomplished what we set out to do. They'll never stop O'Keefe from getting back to Del Norte. The only question is whether we can stay alive and get to Del Norte ourselves."

Until the morning light slowly began to find its way into the forest, Stout led them by following the sound of the creek toward its falls above them. They worked their way back up through the forest by essentially retracing the same path that they'd taken into the forest the night before. As the morning light grew, the men could see that they were shrouded in a heavy fog that felt wet against their faces. But the snow that had fallen through the night was now stopped, and Stout made a comment that the fog would likely burn off and later in the morning the sky should open up for a clear day.

Turner found that walking started to waken his limbs and that once the blood was circulating, he felt warmer. In pauses where Stout would stop to look ahead and find the right way forward, Turner wiggled his toes to keep his feet awake.

When they reached the edge of the timber line, having climbed quite a ways, they saw that their tracks from the night before were completely covered in the fresh snowfall.

"We could wait them out, Lieutenant," Stout said. "If you want, we could go back to that cabin and probably hole up there for a day or two without being found. We'd likely never see those men again."

Turner shook his head.

"I cannot do that," he said. "I'd be ducking my responsibility."

Stout grunted an affirmative response. It was the decision he expected from the young man, but he thought he'd at least give him the choice.

Turner, for his part, was no less resolved than when he'd first turned back to face the men who had slaughtered his command. He did not say it aloud to Stout, but Turner had decided that if he saw these men again – when he saw them again – he intended to engage them, and he would do it without Stout if he had to.

- 27 -

Jacob Stallings dragged the wool blanket up around his neck. The blanket was wet and heavy with snow. He shivered violently. He could not remember a time when his fingers and toes felt so cold. The men of the outfit had tied their horses in a line up near the granite face of an enormous outcropping, and they'd huddled down under blankets pressed up against the rock wall where they hoped to stay out of the wind. And largely they had managed it. The wind did not molest them so much, but the snow fell on them through the night and buried them in frigid cocoons.

"I've not slept a wink," one of the men down the line

muttered as the first gray light of dawn appeared high in the sky. Diffused through the fog, the dawn came in like gray glow more than a light, but the men could now see a little something, and so they began to stir.

They'd been caught out, exposed through the night in the alpine tundra, just as Jacob Stallings feared they would be. There'd been an argument about thirty minutes before dark when the last of dusk still offered some ability to see – some favored turning back while others said they should push forward, but by then it was too late. The snow was falling already, and they all knew that a miserable night was all they had in store for themselves. A few of the hardier sorts were able to doze some with their backs against the rock and their heads on their chests, but most of them spent the night sniffling, coughing, and miserably trying to find a way to manufacture warmth where there was none.

But the sniffling and the coughing was not the only noise through the night.

Jacob Stallings remained keenly aware through the interminable darkness that conversations were taking place up against the cold granite cliff face. Hushed voices, grumbling under their breath, one man speaking quietly to his nearest neighbors. These veterans who Lou Stallings always swore would go where they were told and do what they were told without complaint spent the night lodging their complaints.

They'd been mute to the slaughter of a party of prospectors. They'd said nothing when Lou Stallings told them to rush in and murder a patrol of cavalry troopers. But they rebelled at being led into a night of frigid misery.

The first light of dawn did not assuage the anger, either.

Their many mumbled mutinies were set aside as the men began to stir, but the furtive, angry looks were everywhere. As Jacob shook the snow from his blanket and stretched his legs in preparation for standing, he caught one of the men glaring at him. He saw another grit his teeth and clench his jaw as he glowered at Lou. Jacob Stallings stomped his feet against the rock to shake off the numbness and then went to his brother. Men around them were beginning to saddle their horses while others tried to rub life into their own limbs or into their horses' shoulders.

"We've got a problem," he muttered.

"I've noticed," Lou snapped back. "We'll get moving and that'll stop the grumbling."

There would be no coffee, no breakfast other than cold jerky. They had no fuel for fire out here, though Jacob Stallings would have been grateful for a fire. A few of them ate jerky from their saddlebags while others put leads on their horses and walked around to try to get warm.

"We'll walk the horses," Lou Stallings called out.

The snow had covered all the loose rock covering the ground, and it would be too easy for a horse to stumble, spill a rider or break a leg. Lou wasn't in any mood to compound their troubles. So they would walk the horses.

They went maybe two miles before the terrain began to break precipitously and drop down steep cliffs into little valleys. They saw a cluster of evergreens, and Lou Stallings thought that if they'd gone just a bit farther and come across this tiny cluster of trees, they might have had a better night – shelter and fire and coffee. He cursed their luck that they didn't make it another couple of miles and find this cluster of trees.

"Take Dicky Cort and walk over to those trees," Lou said to his brother. "Check it out and make sure our cavalrymen aren't hiding out there."

Jacob frowned, but he did what his older brother said. Lou and the others kept moving along the ridge, but they were never out of sight of Jacob and Dicky. The two men walked a half circle around the cluster of trees, but they saw no evidence that anyone had camped there. They rejoined the others half a mile farther along the ridge, and they weren't long before coming to a mountain lake. A stream dropped from the lake, and though there was still a thin layer of fog, they could see down below them where the stream entered a forest of pine and cedar.

"They might have followed that stream," Lou suggested, giving voice to his thoughts as much as talking to anyone in particular. Lou wandered a little ways toward the forest, looking it over. It was a big forest and dropped down the west side of the mountain. If they stayed on the trail they were on, they would wind their way down to that forest. From his vantage at the precipice of the ridge, Lou could see how the mountain fell away into a deep canyon. With a pair of wings, he could get to the mountain peak across the valley in the blink of an eye, but it would take a day or more to get there by walking down into the valley and up the next mountain. Either way, Lou Stallings had already decided he would not be going much farther. The day looked to be clearing, but if another snowstorm rolled in, and if it kept snowing, they could easily find this pass inaccessible. They might well have to reach a new plan.

Lou stood for a long time looking at the trees below, and the men started to get restless as they stood, holding their horses. After several minutes, Jacob Stalling approached his brother.

"What are you thinking?" Jacob asked.

"I'm thinking that if I was those cavalrymen, I'd be inside that tree line down below looking at me looking for them."

Jacob felt a chill run up his spine, and not from the cold.

"Do you think they're there?"

"Might well be," Lou said. "This trail we're following, it'll lead below to cabins. My guess, these three men we're chasing bedded down in some prospector's cabin inside those trees. They probably woke up this morning thinking they'd double back on us. I'm going to take a couple of the men and go on down this trail a little ways to see if I can find some sign of them. You're going wait here and make sure they don't get by. Go and fetch some wood, make up a fire if you want to stay warm, and you cover this trail. I wouldn't think we'd be more than a couple of hours getting back here.:

"And if you don't find any sign of them and I don't see them?" Jacob asked.

"Then we're going to hope they froze to death somewhere last night and we're going to make for Del Norte before the weather turns worse."

***

Lou Stallings put a hand over the fire pit inside the cabin. It was cool, but the cabin smelled strong of smoke, the scent was undeniably fresh.

"They camped here in this cabin last night," Lou said.

The hoof prints on the dirt floor solidified his opinion. They'd seen the cabin when the trail met the creek, and though there were no tracks in the snow leading out to the trail, Lou decided to check it out anyway. He found tracks – two men and a horse – leading out of the cabin and then up behind it. He found the fresh makings of a fire. Some of the unburned firewood stacked beside the rock fire pit was still wet – recently brought into the cabin. The cedar branches stuffed into the cabin's walls to break the wind had been hastily put there and were intended to be only a temporary reprieve from the wind.

Lou and the two men he brought with him carried rifles and six-shooters, but they'd left their horses back with the others. Horses would only impede them if it came to a chase through the woods.

"We've got them," Lou said to the others. "We can follow their tracks directly to them, and I guarantee they're going to be caught between us and the others up on the ridge."

He pointed the rifle into the air and fired off a shot that burst through the quiet morning. He hoped that his brother would hear the shot and understand its significance.

Lou Stallings licked his lips as he stood at the back of the cabin, his eyes searching the dark places of the forest.

"We've got them," he said again. "Let's go."

Together, the three men set off, following the tracks in the snow that led away from the cabin and back up the slope. Lou figured at most it would take them three-quarters of an hour to reach the edge of the forest. They would just have to be careful that they didn't come up on men who were waiting for them.

- 28 -

Sergeant O'Keefe sipped from the tip cup. The half-breed scout was gone when he woke, but O'Keefe did not think the man had been gone long. He'd left a kettle on a rock near the fire, and the milky liquid inside was hot. O'Keefe stirred the liquid with his knife and stabbed out what looked like pasty strands of tree flesh. The taste was not bad, but whatever concoction Tommy Irons had given him did seem to have an effect on the pain. Or maybe it was the mixture he'd put on the wound.

At any rate, O'Keefe felt better as he stirred with the morning light.

A thick fog permeated the valley. Though he could

hear it, Sergeant O'Keefe could not see the river. It seemed hard to believe this was the Rio Grande. O'Keefe knew that in Texas, near the mouth, steamboats traveled some way up the river. But here, the river was not deep enough to float a canoe in many places, and along much of the river as he'd passed it, O'Keefe could easily toss a stone from one bank to the other. There would be no steamships coming to his rescue on this Rio Grande.

Hobbled as he was, O'Keefe moved as fast as he could manage to get the horse saddled, not rushed, but eager. He was ready to get on the way. He knew if there were men behind him, he'd put distance between him and them, but the half-breed had caught him. Others could catch him, too. And he still had the lieutenant to think of. Somehow, O'Keefe believed that Stout would survive this. The scouts had that sort of reputation among the troopers, though. The scouts survived when troopers were killed. As proof of the hypothesis, O'Keefe considered that his men had all been killed, but Stout was still out there. Even if Lieutenant Turner would be killed, Levi Stout would make it back to Del Norte, Sergeant O'Keefe believed this.

There'd been a light dusting of snow overnight – nothing that would impede travel – and the fog added a chill to the air. But after a decent night's sleep and the medicinal tea Tommy Irons boiled in the kettle, O'Keefe felt a renewed strength to get back on the trail.

He gathered up the leads for the other horses and pulled them along as he got his mount started. When the horses were all moving, he tied off their leads and let them move on ahead of him. They followed the trail without giving him any trouble. They were good cavalry horses and did what was asked of them.

The valley here along the Rio Grande provided plenty of flat ground for an easy ride, surrounded by big hills to the left and right, the river ambling over its rocky bottom and making a pretty song that reminded the Irishman of the slip jigs of his homeland, graceful and chaotic and flowing on and on.

For a trooper who'd journeyed through the dry grasslands of upper Texas and the Nations, and down through the desert of New Mexico Territory, the crystal-clear song of the mountain river constantly making music by his trail offered a sense of security. At any point if his canteen ran dry, he could pull reins and dip that canteen into the river and come up with cold, fresh water. Sergeant O'Keefe decided he'd take a wounded leg beside a river over a hundred miles of dry territory any day.

"Ridin' into Del Norte by dark, we'll be," O'Keefe said to the horse, and the note of happiness in his voice surprised even himself.

"Might have been a drop of whiskey in that Indian's concoction," he mused. "It's no wonder I'm feelin' more like meself than I have for days."

The horses seemed to be feeling all right, too. O'Keefe kept them at a good lope through most of the morning, reining in at times to spare the horses a bit, and changing mounts a couple of times in the morning, though that seemed excessive.

By noon, the sergeant was wishing he had more of Tommy Irons' concoction that might ease back the pain some as his leg began to throb, but he decided that throbbing was better than the complete numbness that he'd experienced the previous day. So he drove on, keeping the horses moving at a good clip and wondering how the lieutenant and scout were faring.

- 29 -

"Was that a shot?" Lieutenant Turner asked, turning sharply to look back through the woods in the direction the noise had come.

The fog was mostly burned off now, though some wisps still clung in the trees. Stout had been expecting trouble from behind for some time now. He and the lieutenant had watched from within the darkness of the timber line as the men up on the ridge broke into two parties, three men going ahead on a trail that Stout knew would lead them to the cabin. A couple of the men from the ridge came down to the woods. Turner suggested that would be the time to fall upon them with knives and begin thinning the numbers against them. Stout considered it, but then a third man armed with a rifle came a little ways down the ridge to guard the first two. He stood out in the open where he could not be got at without exposing themselves to the other men up on the ridge – or with a rifle shot that would alert the three who'd gone on down the trail.

In a short while, the two men in the woods reemerged with armfuls of branches and twigs, and up on the ridge they built up a fire. The men on the ridge then crowded around the fire. A half dozen of them, plus the three who went on down the trail. At least now they knew how many men they faced as adversaries.

"It was a shot," Stout said.

"They've found the cabin," Turner said.

Stout nodded, but his eyes were on the men on the ridge. They'd all been standing around the fire. Earlier, right after they'd built the fire, they'd made first one pot of coffee and then a second, and most of them were holding coffee cups still. The shot started new activity. A couple of men set down their coffee pots and took up rifles.

"They'll be coming up behind us," Turner said. "We'll be trapped between the men behind us in the woods and those up on the ridge."

Stout guessed that the shot was fired down at the cabin. Following their tracks in the light of the morning, the men down in the woods would make good time. They'd be behind them in half an hour.

"Let's get moving," Stout said.

He led the way, turning back from the trail and trying to find a path that might allow them to get in behind the men up on the ridge. Instinct told him such a trail existed.

But however they went, they would be easy to follow. Their tracks in the snow were as obvious as guideposts or blazes on trees. They could not backtrack along the creek in the hopes of hiding their tracks because the shoals and drops would prove too difficult to maneuver. But they did have to cross the creek. Now the trick was finding a route that would take them beyond the lake where the creek originated. Stout's memory of the trip in from the day before told him that if they could get above the lake, they would not be seen by the men down on the ridge. They'd wasted too much time watching the men on the ridge, and Stout silently cursed himself now for having stood so long. He'd been waiting for those men to press forward or to wander, but they'd built the fire at the precipice of the ridge and they'd stayed near it.

The forest wrapped around the contour of the mountain, and they soon found themselves facing a steep, bare drop – too steep for even the snow to cling to.

"We can climb here at the edge of the cliff," Stout said. "But I think when we reach the top of this slope we'll be in sight of the men on the ridge."

"Unless we're going to shoot our way through them, this is the only option," Turner said.

"Those others in the woods will be on us in a matter of minutes if we start shooting," Stout said.

"Then lead the way up the slope."

They emerged from the timberline and followed the slope just along the edge of the precipitous drop. The shape of the upper ridge beyond the waterfall protected them from the view of those men above, but if the men coming up from behind reached the tree line and looked out this way, they'd be seen for sure.

As they climbed up toward the ridge, making a series of switchback turns in the snow to make the slope manageable, Stout eyed the cliff face that dropped below them. Right away, he spotted a ledge that wrapped around the cliff. It was narrow in places, hardly wide enough for a man to shimmy across with his belly pressed up against the cliff face, but in other spots it was wide enough for two men to walk it side-by-side. Stout could not see how far it went, but if it were not for the horse, that ledge might make a route of escape. The snow clung to the ledge only in patches. If they were careful, they might even be able to navigate the ledge without ever leaving a track.

Stout already had a plan in mind – getting beyond that small mountain lake out of sight of the men on the ridge and then making a run back the way they'd come the previous day. But in his mind, he marked that ledge as another option. He knew, as any good scout did, that survival often meant watching the landscape for fresh options.

They reached the top of the ridge without being seen, but what they found there wasn't helpful.

From their present position, the men farther down the ridge couldn't see the lieutenant and the scout. A large hill this side of the creek protected them from view. But if they tried to work around the far side of the lake, they'd be fully exposed to those men.

Stout took a heavy breath of the crisp air.

"We don't have much choice in this, and there's no time to argue about it," Stout said. "In a few minutes, those men coming from behind us will figure out where we are, and we won't have long once they do. So I'm going to go back down this slope and draw their attention. When I do, and when it's clear, you get on this horse and ride back down that trail we took yesterday. You can find it?"

"I can find it," Turner said, "but I'm not leaving you here to face these men alone."

"You'll have others to face," Stout said. "They've only brought some of their outfit after us, which means the rest of them are probably somewhere between here and Del Norte. Maybe they've caught up with Sergeant O'Keefe, or maybe not. But if they have, then you're the only one who can roundup a posse in Del Norte. There's no time to argue with me. Watch for your chance and be ready to move out."

Stout reached into the saddlebag and drew out a box of cartridges for his rifle. He dropped those into the possibles bag slung over his shoulder, and then he descended the slope. He followed the tracks they'd made coming up the slope, and he went as fast as he could manage.

***

Stout knew where to look, and he saw the men making their way through the forest – just three shadows moving inside the dark shroud of the trees. But they were following the tracks that Stout, the lieutenant, and the horse had made, and so Stout knew where they would be.

He was down behind a boulder, but in just a few minutes those men would appear outside the trees, and they would see him. They would see the tracks leading up to the ridge. Now was the time.

Stout raised up his rifle and aimed into the woods, seeking out one of those shadows. They weren't more than forty yards away now, and he led them with the rifle, waiting for them to get close enough that he could be absolutely sure of the shot. In moments, he would be in a shootout with nine men, his back to a drop of fifty feet or more, and he wanted to make this first shot count for something.

He let out a breath, put the smallest pressure on the trigger, waited for the shadows to appear inside that space where he was aiming, where no tree would interrupt the lead.

And when one of those shadows darkened the space behind the sight, Levi Stout put more pressure on the trigger.

The Winchester barked and echoed. The shadow in the woods jerked and stumbled and fell back.

Stout did not wait to watch what happened next. He stood up from behind the boulder, exposing himself so that he would be seen, and quickly worked the lever on the Winchester to chamber another round. He fired off one more round into the woods, knowing he would not hit anything. This second shot didn't matter. This was just to be sure he got the attention of the men up on the ridge.

Someone in the woods shot back, but Stout was already moving now, going out onto that ledge he'd seen earlier.

Another shot behind him, and they were shouting.

"They're down here!" someone yelled.

Stout did not turn to look, he knew the men from the woods were shouting to the men up on the ledge, calling down the others to help.

The army scout moved quickly where he could, where

the ledge was wider, and got to a bend in the cliff face. He was now at least a little protected from anyone shooting at him from the slope. Now he was about fifteen yards out onto the cliff face, working his way around. Here the ledge began to narrow, and he had to hug the rock to avoid falling.

A rifle shot thundered behind him and chips of the rock from over his head rained down on him, bouncing off the brim of his hat. Another rifle shot, more pebbles clattering off his hat, but they couldn't get a shot at him.

Stout heard the men shouting, calling for the others to come and help.

He shimmied another five feet farther around the face of the rock, and that's where Levi Stout ran out of ledge. He'd gone as far as he could go.

"Can you see him?" he heard one of the men demand of the other.

"He's around that bend there," came the answer.

"Go out there after him."

"Like hell. I ain't going out there."

Stout had one hand on his rifle and the other hand gripped a small crevice in the granite. He just needed to last out here for ten minutes. If he could make it fifteen, that would be better.

Clinging to the escarpment, waiting for those men behind him to figure out how they were going to get at him, Stout began to think now about Faustina. He still wanted to find some way back to her. Now he was trying to buy the lieutenant time to get away, but the man yearned to survive. A man with a good woman at home has much yet to live for, and Stout was in no hurry to give up those cold nights pressed against his wife's warm body, or evenings on the front porch, smoking a cigar and watching the stars pass by and listening to her laughter as they talked of nothing. Children. He'd never been the sort of man to think much about children, but since he'd married Faustina and left the regular employ of the army, that dream had sprouted. He was still young enough for that, to be a father, to dream of things he'd not before dreamed of.

He set the rifle down on the ledge, pressed between himself and the rock face, and reached into his pocket for a string. He looped the string around his belt and then, with just one hand, tied the string into the rifle's saddle ring. He doubled checked his knot to be sure it was secure, and then he worked the loop around to the back of his belt so that the rifle hung off of him like a rigid tail. He slid off his leather gloves and dropped them into the possibles sack hanging from his shoulder. If he was going to get out of this, he would have to climb out.

The rifle, hanging down behind his legs, clattered against the rock wall as Stout reached up with his right foot, tested a small foothold and then shifted his weight onto his right foot, pushing himself high enough where he could reach into a crevice and gain a hold with his fingers.

That first moment of literally clinging to the side of the cliff gave the man a sudden sense of regret – the strain on his leg, the ache in his fingers clinging to the rock, the dizzying height, and that moment of realization that all that was between him and plummeting was the two points of contact with the rock, foot and fingers, and the strength of his limbs. He laid his face against the rock as if that was another hold and almost lost his hat. He swept it off his head with his free hand and tucked it into the straps of his possibles bag. If it fell, it fell.

He laid flat against the rock face, his left leg hanging useless in the air, his left hand pressed against the rock without a hold. The rock was cold as ice against his cheek as he tilted his head back, looking for the next spot in his ascension.

The tiny ledge where he stood was only large enough for him to get the toes of his left foot on, but with both feet on the ledge, he found the next foothold to shift to. It would have to be like this, working his right hand and foot into holds, onto small ledges, wherever he could get them, and then his left hand and foot, constantly shifting right as he hugged the escarpment.

A crack in the wall of rock, just wide enough for him to wedge a foot into, gave him the next foothold. His hand found purchase inside that same crack.

A long, narrow ledge overhead gave him the next handhold. He curled his fingers over the edge of it. He dislodged his foot from the crack and blindly felt with the toe of his boot for some place where he could get find a landing. He had to stretch far so that his left foot was only touching the crack, no longer wedged into it, but he found a rock jutting out from the side of the cliff face and put weight on it, but his foot slipped. For a moment, Stout thought he would go over – all his weight suspended just by the curled fingers of his two hands. His left foot shot back into the crack, finding it instinctively. He breathed for a moment. All his muscles seemed strained to the point of breaking. Everything in his body was taut and aching. He'd only come a little ways and still would have to find a way to ascend the cliff, but already he felt that the strain would exhaust him.

He could hear voices behind him. Those men seemed to still be arguing about whether one of them would follow him out onto the ledge, and which one it would be. He thought it must be more than just the two men. He hoped they'd all come off that ridge and given the lieutenant the opening he needed to make an escape. If not, this was all embarrassingly foolish.

He had to reach up with his right foot so that his knee was bent above his waist, but he found a foothold, and this was a strong one. Once he stood up on it, it would put his head level with the ledge he was holding. Now he could shimmy his hands along the ledge and find places to park his feet, and the going got easier, and soon Stout had worked close to twenty yards farther along the face of the cliff, and it curved in such a way that he could only just see the ledge where he'd made the decision to climb. Still none of the other men had come out.

If they tried to get below to the bottom of the cliff to shoot up at him, they'd be twenty or thirty minutes getting down there. Stout did not think they could get above him. The escarpment rose high up over the ridge where he'd left the lieutenant, and up there the slope looked like the edge of a bowl, flat and smooth. There'd be no way up above him, not from the ridge, anyway.

He'd heard no shots that weren't aimed at him – nothing from that ridge up by the lake. That was a good sign. Either they'd not seen the lieutenant as he'd made his escape or he was still hunkered down and out of sight where Stout had left him. If it was the latter, they'd find him soon enough. But if it was the former, Stout's climb was giving him time.

The cliff face slanted up ahead at enough of an angle that Stout could flatten himself against the rock without fear of falling, and plenty of rocks jutted out into tiny ledges where he could get a hold with his hands or find a pedestal for his feet. Here the going got easier, and Stout was able to move freely higher up the cliff face.

The next bit would be difficult. Stout had worked himself out maybe forty yards from the slope, and possibly ten or fifteen feet higher, where the men were gathered, and the curve of the cliff face had taken him away from them, out of their sight, but now the cliff jutted back out and at least for a few minutes as he tried to navigate that portion of the rock face, he was going to be fully exposed.

- 30 -

Elliot Turner wanted to make some argument, but Stout disappeared over the crest of the ridge so fast that he'd had no time to protest.

He had been the one willing to sacrifice himself so that the sergeant and the scout could make for Del Norte. It was Turner who faced the prospect of a court martial and humiliation, and it was Turner who'd deemed that sacrifice was preferable to disgrace. And now, without a moment for debate, the lieutenant found himself in the position of having to flee while another man committed what should have been his sacrifice. It seemed just one more failure of his first – and almost certainly, last –

command.

But Turner also knew that he had to do as Stout instructed. The mission had to be finished, and his sacrifice might not be his life, but his future.

He heard the shots from below, and the shouting, and more shots. He had to fight the urge to take a look to see what was happening. He stayed back, away from the lip of the ridge so as not to expose himself. He waited, giving the other men time to come down off the ridge. Likely they would leave one or two to keep the horses, but Stout clearly counted on those men to be distracted.

He could hear the chaos below as other men began to arrive. They'd been confounded. They argued over something, and Turner expected it was some argument about going out on the ledge.

And then a shout, "There! He's come around!"

Turner understood that Stout must have been out of their sight, but now they had him again. And that's when the shots started. A sole rifle shot echoed out across the big valley below. Then a second, followed by a close third.

"Now's the time," Turner said to the horse.

He stepped out toward the lake, taking big steps through the snow, tugging the lead to keep the horse moving with him. And then he was out, beyond the hill that had protected him from view, making his way along the slope on the far side of the lake.

He did not look at first, worried that he would somehow give away his own presence by looking out across the lake, as if by not looking at whatever other men might be over there, they would also not look at him. But at last he slowed his strides and allowed the horse to come up even with him, walking beside the animal so that it was between him and the lake and the men on the other side. And then, at last, Turner chanced a look over the horse's back, out across the lake.

Indeed, there were nine horses picketed in the snow not far from where a smoke continued to rise from a campfire. Near the horses, but looking down the ridge toward the creek, toward the cliff face, Turner counted three men. That meant there were still six down lower, and that none of them had emerged suggested to Turner that Stout was still alive, still giving them trouble. Even as the thought occurred to him, he heard another shot shortly followed by a second. The second shot told him the first had not done its job, but the absence of a third shot worried him. Had they finally gotten Stout?

At some point, someone down below the ridge was going to notice the tracks leading up the ridge and figure out that Stout was alone. That would be the critical moment. There would be no sneaking past then. Turner would have to mount and ride, and he would have to ride hard. He thought of how rocky the terrain was up here, how easy it would be for the horse to hit a loose rock buried under the snow and throw him, or step into a hidden hole. So for now he walked, making as much distance as he could.

Turner edged around the lake. His steps were calm but deliberate. Innately, he understood that a galloping horse would draw attention where a wandering horse might not. He'd managed to put a quarter of a mile between him and the ridge, possibly farther than that, when at last he heard renewed shouting behind and he turned to see a man at the crest of the ridge, twisted around to shout to the men below. Turner gave a tug on the cinch, tightening it, and secured it with a knot. Then he stepped into the saddle, giving one more look behind as he did. The man at the ridge was raising up a rifle now.

"Get up," Turner said to the horse, and the beast was equal to the test. Its legs warmed up from the walk, the horse moved quickly from walk to lope and the shot, when it came, came harmless.

The horse moved out across the bank of the lake as sure-footed as it could be, and Turner developed an appreciation for his new mount. Raised in the mountains, well-acquainted with the rugged terrain, the animal did not miss a step. Turner kept his eyes ahead, locked on the long ridge that stretched out across the tundra. As he rounded the lake and came to the trail, he'd top a hill and be out of sight of the men behind him. If Stout was still alive there would be a least a few minutes of confusion. Would they divide their force yet again? Who would pursue? Who would stay to try to deal with Stout? If Turner could get beyond the hill, he'd have a clear run back to the Del Norte road, and today he was mounted.

- 31 -

Levi Stout picked up his left foot and held it suspended in the air for a moment. Then he pressed it back against the wall. He'd worked himself into a crevice, his feet locked in on one side, his back pressed firm on the other. If he shifted at all, he'd be back within sight and easy rifle range of the men behind him. Two or three of them had come out on the ledge as far as they could go and still have room to shoulder their rifles. They'd taken a few shots at him, but all they'd done was chipped a piece of rock that hit him in the eye and gave him fits.

But now the fits came from his exhausted muscles. Climbing out across this rock face had cost him considerable strain. His entire body ached, not least his ankles as his feet pressed hard against the rock.

"Is your name Stout?" one of the men on the ledge called, breaking for a moment his thoughts of pain. Stout frowned, but surely Tommy Irons had given his name.

"That's right."

"Falling off this cliff would be a helluva way to die."

"That it would," Stout agreed. "Who're you that I'm talking to?"

"My name is Lou Stallings." That Stallings was willing to give away his name told Stout they had no intention of allowing him to live. "Why don't you work your way back over here and let's, you and me, talk this over. Maybe you don't have to die on them rocks below."

"I expect I've got better odds with the rocks," Stout called back.

"Maybe, but if you don't come on back here, we won't know that."

The crevice widened as it rose, but he could work his way deeper into it and continue to climb, feet and back pressing against the walls of the crevice. But he still had maybe twenty feet to go to reach the crest. If he could get there, he would have to see the terrain and then try to decide what was next. Another climb down, possibly, or maybe he'd find a trail that might lead some way other than back down to the lake.

Stout pressed his shoulders into the wall behind him and stepped with first one foot and then the next. Then he pressed his arms into the wall behind him and lunged up. Climbing twenty feet like this, six inches at a time, seemed an impossible task.

"When you fall down out of there, is there anyone you want us to write a letter to?" Lou Stallings shouted.

That's when a fresh eruption of shouting came from farther back. Stout couldn't make out what they were saying, but he suspected someone had at last seen the lieutenant making his escape.

Stout shimmied a little ways deeper inside the crevice, staying away from where it opened wider above him. Then he took a heavy breath and worked his way up another six inches. The rock seemed to be stabbing into his back. He reached around, trying to find a handhold where he could take some of the pressure off of his back, at least for a moment. The crevice widened above him, but beside him it narrowed until it finally closed off. He reached into this narrow gap and was able to find a good handhold. Now he hoisted himself up another foot, and then another. Now he worked one foot into the tight part of the crevice until it was wedged thoroughly, and then he reached again for another handhold. When he found one, he had four points touching the rock – one foot pressed against the crevice wall and the other wedged into the narrow portion of the crevice, his fingers on the handhold, and his back pressed against the other wall of the crevice. It was the most secure he'd felt since he'd come off the ledge.

Working like this, he managed to get himself another foot higher, and then another, and in a moment, he'd managed to get high enough that the crevice began to slope back. Two more feet, and then another three feet, and Stout was able to set his feet on the slope and carefully bear-walk up it, using both hands to keep himself from slipping back.

"Hey! Are you coming out of there or not?" Lou Stallings shouted, and a tension in the man's voice suggested to Stout that they'd lost sight of him and did not know that he'd managed to find a path up. They fired another shot into the crevice, but this one hit well below where Stout was climbing.

And then he was out – free of the crevice and free of the cliff. He found himself now perched on a narrow but manageable ridge with a commanding view overlooking the valley far below, the forest where he'd camped and, on the other side, the lake. Tracks in the snow suggested that Lieutenant Turner had managed to at least get out to the distant hill unmolested.

Stout dropped to a crouch, hoping no one below could see him, and he moved fast along the ridge. Ahead of him, the rocky ridge sloped up, meeting that hill where Turner had disappeared. That would have to be his way out, and he would have to beat Stallings and his men there. He was on foot and they would be mounted, and there was small chance he could beat them.

- 32 -

"Is he still in there?" Dicky Cort asked, craning his neck and stepping as close to the edge of the ledge as he could comfortably do.

"I don't know," Lou Stallings grumbled. Everything just kept getting worse. When they'd first spotted the man out on the ledge, they thought they had all three of them, assuming the other two had gone farther out. But then Stout climbed around and exposed himself. Stallings took a couple of shots at the man, but Stallings never had been the best shot and he'd always been queasy with heights. He was too nervous to hold his gun steady. Then the scout worked himself into the crevice, out of view. That's when

Lou Stallings realized they'd been hoodwinked, and he sent Dicky Cort to the top of the ridge, and Dicky saw one of them riding off.

There were moments of confusion. Dicky was up on the ridge and Lou was out here on the ledge. It was Jacob who came out and told Lou what was going on.

"They split up," Jacob said. "One of them's riding off."

"Where's the other one?" Lou asked, though he knew Jacob didn't know the answer. Lou spit forth a string of expletives as his brother stood mute before him.

Jacob Stallings was beginning to believe their expedition was ill-fated. Everything seemed to be going against them.

"What are we going to do?"

Lou shook his head, depleted after the miserable night they'd spent. The others had stood by a fire, but Lou still hadn't gotten warm.

"If Tommy Irons was here, he'd go out on that cliff and put a bullet in that man," Lou said angrily. He said the comment loud enough that everyone around would hear, hoping that maybe one of them would work up the nerve to do what Lou wouldn't do himself. But no volunteers stepped forward.

Instead, Jacob said, "What about the one up above, riding away?"

"Take Dicky and someone else and ride after him," Lou said with a nod toward the upper ridge. "I'll stay here to deal with this one."

Not wanting to test his brother's anger, Jacob turned abruptly and hurried off the ledge. He grabbed Dicky Cort and another man they called Texas Eddie to differentiate him from the other Eddie who was now lying dead in the woods, the victim of the scout's first rifle shot of the morning.

Though the three men hurried, there was nothing fast about what they did. They had to make it from the ledge over the creek and up the ridge. In the time it took for them to saddle their horses and check their weapons, the horseman had disappeared over the distant hill.

They left behind five men, now that the other Eddie was killed, three down on the ledge and two standing with the horses. The last Jacob Stallings said the men with the horses was that they would meet up with the others of their outfit, those waiting down on the road to Del Norte.

"You tell my brother we'll be waiting there for you," Jacob said.

Dicky Cort was already off, out ahead. Mostly, Dicky just wanted this whole thing to be over. Like the others, he'd spent a miserable night in the cold. He was angry over the way this had gone. He didn't mind killing the prospectors, nor did he much care about killing the soldiers. But Lou Stallings had mishandled this job, and Dicky was just about done being told what to do by Lou Stallings or anyone else. He wanted to collect his wages and move on. If he had a penny to his name, he'd have moved on already.

So Dicky rode hard and soon left Jacob Stallings and Texas Eddie behind, even though he'd heard Jacob twice call for him to wait up.

Dicky topped the hill and saw the cavalryman out ahead of him, maybe half a mile or more. He was just loping up over the next hill. Dicky tried to remember the route they'd come the day before. At some point, that cavalryman would come even with the cluster of evergreens. Then it was maybe a couple of miles before he reached the saddle and then down into the forest, working his way along the trail that ran down to the Del Norte road. It was along that trail that a lot of prospectors had built their cabins and done their digging during the summer, on all the mountain streams that ran down into the valley and fed the Rio Grande.

It would be best if they could catch up to the cavalryman here on the tundra. In the forest there were too many places to hide. He could abandon the horse and take to the woods. So Dicky Cort gave the horse a couple of quick taps on the rump with the reins, but the horse still wouldn't get moving any faster.

"Damned horses are just as cold as we are," Dicky shouted to no one in particular.

It seemed that every time Dicky topped a ridge where he was in sight of the cavalryman, the man was already approaching the crest of the next hill.

If he couldn't catch him, Dicky wanted at least to keep the man in sight.

- 33 -

Levi Stout sat down with his back against the wide trunk of a tall pine. He shut his eyes and wrapped his arms around himself against the cold. The sun had finally broken through the fog, but under the canopy of the trees he found almost no comfort from the sun. His muscles ached and he desperately wanted to eat. He had a little jerky in his bag, but he'd decided against eating that now. He might need it more later.

After running along the ridge, Stout found a deer path that dropped down off the ridge and into a forest. It would put him miles away from the path down to the Del Norte road, miles away from Lieutenant Turner. But he saw no opportunity now to be of any help to the lieutenant. The man was on his own. Now, Stout decided, he would work to save himself.

He had a knack for finding his way through terrain where he'd never been before. When he'd scouted for the army against the Indians, he used to claim he was like a horse, he could always find the trail home. But he was turned around now and not certain how he would work his way back. He also had no idea if Stallings and those other men would track him. It seemed doubtful that they would give up. From the ridge he'd seen the tracks in the snow below that told him some of them had given chase after the lieutenant, but he knew at least four or five of them had stayed behind. It wouldn't take them long to figure out that he'd escaped that crevice on the cliff. They'd find his tracks in the snow up on the ridge, but they'd play hell getting up there. They'd have to climb to the ridge from the lake, and that wouldn't be easy. That slope going up to the high ridge from the lake was steep. It would be easier than the climb Stout made, certainly, but they wouldn't be able to do it quickly. Tracking him along the ridge would be no problem. He'd left prints in the snow, but that couldn't be helped. They'd have a harder time in the woods. There was less snow accumulated here, and no clear trail. He avoided leaving tracks wherever he could, but there were large patches of snow that he could not avoid. He might have left a trail hard to follow, but he'd left a trail all the same.

A moment's rest. He just needed to shut his eyes for a few moments, catch his breath, and then he would get moving again.

He'd been scared out on the ledge and afraid in that crevice, and that was a hard thing to admit to himself. Stout thought of himself as a competent man and that was what he put out into the world. Whether on horseback or tracking through the woods, or shooting a rifle – all these things that a man needed to do to survive on the rough frontier, Levi Stout made himself competent at these things. Fear interrupted competency, and he did not want to be afraid.

But on that ledge, climbing that crevice, he felt full of fear. He had to shake that off. He did not fear men tracking him. He could handle men. What he could not handle was his limbs giving out and plummeting to the rocks below.

Most of all, he wanted now to find his way home.

He used his rifle to push himself off the ground and then started back through the woods. He worked himself lower as he went. Even if he turned up miles away, he had to work his way down to the valley where he would find the Del Norte road.

Stout followed the contour of the land, dropping lower through the forest. He found a draw and followed that until it paid out on a flat ridge. He was moving to the south and east, generally, and he knew that was the direction that would take him toward the Del Norte road. What he did not know is what might be between here and there. Would he have to cross another mountain? Would there be a deep gorge in his way that would require climbing or going around? They might have come so far in the tundra up above that he was days away from the road coming this way. But he did not think so. If he had to guess, Stout believed that the road would lie somewhere in the valley below. He thought probably he would have to cross some hills and maybe a little tough terrain. If there was a gorge, he'd try to get around it.

The morning slipped away into afternoon as the army scout made his way through the forest. He'd had no sign to suggest that anyone had come in pursuit of him.

Late in the day, Stout entered a mountain meadow and for the first time had a clear view of the terrain around him. He'd descended quite a distance down the mountain, and he could see now that the valley below was wide with patches of forest, bare hills and a large sandstone butte some miles farther along. He did not have a clear view of the terrain surrounding that butte, but he was almost certain that was the place where the lieutenant and the sergeant had hid the morning after the troopers were ambushed. If he was right and that was the place, he would be at least one more day getting back to it, but that butte was his sole landmark telling him where to find the Del Norte road.

He found a deer path at the opposite end of the meadow, and he followed that. Stout ignored the cold. He ignored his hunger pangs. He ignored the exhaustion in his muscles. He had reached a point where now he was simply trying to survive – survive the elements and survive whatever men might be behind him. But all those skills of a frontiersman at which Levi Stout excelled, they were skills that pointed to one specific purpose: survival. At least up to now, he'd excelled enough that he always survived.

***

Dusk found Levi Stout huddled in a small lean-to he constructed of cedar boughs. He used his knife to dig a shallow hole at the entrance of his shelter and he made up a little fire to give his hands some warmth.

He ate some of his jerky. He'd tried to get a squirrel

with a rock, but all he managed to do was hit the trunk of a tree and scare off the one squirrel he'd seen all afternoon. So it was just a bit of jerky for supper, a little warmth from a small fire. The shelter he made was small and tight and held the warmth from the fire well. He fed it with only small twigs and small lengths of broken branches and never allowed the fire to get so big that it would give him away, but he stayed awake late into the night, continuing to put a few twigs and small branches into the fire so that it kept burning and kept warming his shelter.

All through the day he'd eaten handfuls of snow. Water was more important than food, and water could fool his stomach into believing he was not hungry. At least, that's what he'd been told at some point. In truth, he still felt plenty hungry. The jerky did little to diminish that.

After some time, he stretched his arm out and put his head into his shoulder. He listened to the conversation of the forest – the owls and the wolves, the wind in the tops of the trees. He closed his eyes, they were useless now anyway. The owls told him that no predators were near. Nothing wandered in the darkness of the forest that should not be there. The wolves' distant howling let him know that he was near the valley where they hunted this time of year. The wind moaning in the trees reminded him that morning would break cold and he should slide another branch into his fire pit.

Somewhere in there, the forest stopped talking to him, and Stout fell into the oblivion that would take away some of the ache in his body and give him the strength to face the next day.

- 34 -

Lieutenant Turner swung his leg over the back of the horse and dropped down out of the saddle. Quickly, he looped the reins over the saddle horn and took up the lead rope. He slid the Winchester rifle from its scabbard, and then he carefully stepped off the trail and into the thick of the forest, avoiding mud, avoiding snow, and landing his feet on soft pine straw. He kept the lead rope taut so that as much as possible the horse would follow in his footsteps, finding only a bed of pine straw and no mud.

He'd run the horse out, and the animal had nothing left. It needed sleep and water and probably a good pasture to graze. But the gelding had been equal to the challenge. He never faltered. He never stumbled or missed a step. Through rough terrain, the mountain horse had acquitted himself admirably.

"You keep quiet and watch your step," Turner said, leading the horse deep into the woods. "If they come after us, we'll deal with them."

He'd thought to run the horse out completely, and when the horse could go no farther, Turner thought he might make a stand on the trail. An ambush. But then he'd changed his mind. Stout had said that maybe Sergeant O'Keefe never got to Del Norte, and Turner realized that he would be failing in his duty if he did not see these men brought to justice. So he decided that whatever his worries about a court martial, whatever thoughts he had of dying a valiant death to avoid humiliation, he had to keep going. He had to make certain that the names of Jacob and Lou Stallings were said to men in Del Norte, that warrants were sworn, and that the law came after these men.

And so he drew reins, leapt from the saddle, and now he led the horse into the woods hoping to find a place to hide. He had to let the horse rest because without the horse, he would never make it.

One did not have to go far into the woods to disappear, and when the riders in pursuit passed the spot where Turner and the horse left the trail, they saw nothing of the lieutenant or the horse.

Dicky Cort's horse was equally exhausted, and he'd slowed to a walk. That allowed Jacob Stallings and Texas Eddie to catch up.

"I hate to say this," Dicky said after some time of the three men riding at a walk.

"Hate to say what?" Jacob Stallings asked, a tinge of anger in his voice. Like his brother, Jacob had run all out of patience for things going wrong, and he'd become morose as he reflected over all the mistakes he'd made. The biggest of those, he'd concluded, was putting together this outfit and trying for a big payoff. But below that, there were a dozen other terrible mistakes that plagued him. He did not want to add another to the list, but he already had a premonition of what Dicky Cort was going to say next.

"I don't think we're followin' that trooper no more," Dicky said.

"Why?"

"I don't see no tracks from him," Dicky said.

The trail was not covered over completely in snow the way the tundra had been. It was mostly snow and mud. But even without tracks in the snow to follow, there should have been tracks in the mud. It had been some time now since he'd seen the last track, and he'd long ago lost sight of the cavalryman. The forest contained too many twists and turns for a man riding half a mile behind another man to ever catch sight of him.

"Where could he have gone?" Jacob asked.

"Into the woods," Dicky said. "That's the only thing. We rode past a cabin back a ways. He could have ducked into that cabin."

"Lou's gonna be mighty angry," Jacob observed, but Dicky Cort had no response to that.

"We'd best turn back and try to find where we lost him at," Texas Eddie said.

Jacob pulled the reins on his horse and sat for a while in the middle of the trail. As he thought back, he remembered coming past at least three cabins. They'd passed by a wide meadow, as well. But the meadow had been covered in snow, and if the cavalryman had ridden into that meadow, Jacob was sure he'd have seen the tracks.

"Can you find him?" Jacob asked. "If we turn around, can you find where he left the trail?"

"I can try," Dicky said with a small shrug. "If there's tracks in the mud, I reckon I can see them as well as anyone can."

"But will you see them?" Jacob asked.

"All I can do is try," Dicky said.

Jacob shook his head, his eyes clenched shut. A headache was forming in the center of his forehead. Lou would have a fit if they didn't kill this cavalryman. All pretense was gone now. They wouldn't bother with primitive weapons, trying to make it look like Utes. They'd shoot the cavalryman if they could get sights on him. Hell, Indians had rifles the same as anyone else. But all that mattered now was that they kill this man. Time was running out for the Stallings outfit. They needed to get out of the mountains, file the claim, and then sell it. And this running around up and down the mountains was too much.

"All right," Jacob said after several moments, but he still had not yet unclenched his eyes. "Let's turn back and try to find him."

***

Turner kept going through the woods. The deer path

led him to a creek where he stopped and waited while the horse decided whether or not to drink. When it finished with the water, Turner found a place where he and the horse both could cross the stream without any problem, and on the other side he found another deer path through the woods. This path took him to a wide clearing covered in snow, but the clearing sat at the base of a large rock face, and up close to the wall of rock the ground was clear. So Turner walked the horse up that way and only then did he venture out of the cover of the trees. If his pursuers came across this meadow, they'd have to search it to find tracks. There was no point in making it easy on them.

He realized that he was thinking like the scout. He was not only reading the terrain to find his way, but he was giving thought to what evidence he'd left behind. Still, he was sure that Stout would have done it better. He'd have known that the base of the rock wall would be bare of snow before he even got to it. He'd have made his decisions faster. He might even leave a trail that would confuse the men behind him and buy himself more time to extend his lead on them. But at least he was beginning to think the right way about things, planning out what he would do and, more importantly, being deliberate about why he was doing the things he was doing.

Of course, Stout would probably already be down to the Del Norte road. He'd have found some way to keep the horse going without running the thing into the ground.

Turner wondered if it was always true that the scouts were the true leaders of the cavalry's expeditions. And he wondered why the cavalry even bothered at all with officers when it could just turn command over to men like Levi Stout who knew what they were doing. He cursed now his time at West Point where he had studied the movement of armies and heard lectures on the great commanders and learned about artillery and supplying an army on the move. These lessons seemed useless here in the mountains. What good did it do to know of Hannibal or Agincourt or Gettysburg when he was one man on his own facing a couple dozen men?

What he needed most were lessons on surviving the frontier, where no matter how dangerous the adversary the greater danger was nature itself – the freezing temperatures, the falling snow, the lack of food. It was no use to know how to send a column of men into battle when there was no column of men.

He worked his way around the meadow and on the far side he had no choice but to leave tracks in the snow that showed exactly where he reentered the forest and followed another trail made by animals.

Perhaps it was the darkness of the woods or his own wandering mind, but dusk fell around the lieutenant and took him entirely by surprise. In a narrow draw, he curled up against the ground with his blanket over him, and Stout's blanket on the horse.

He did not sleep, but he dozed through the night, waking often to the sounds of forest creatures screeching or howling. The wind shook the tree tops and toppled piles of snow from the branches.

The lieutenant was cold and miserable, and he wondered now if he'd eaten too much of the jerky in the saddlebags. Maybe he should have saved some.

- 35 -

Benton Folley sat in a halo of light coming down from the lamp hung in the rafters. He took a large drink from his coffee cup and returned it to the table.

The constant, low noise of three dozen drunken men carrying on their conversations was sometimes interrupted by a loud explosion of noise – a spilled mug, a dropped glass, someone at one of the card tables shouting in ecstasy or despair, an unnecessarily loud greeting between two men who hadn't seen each other for weeks or months or maybe just hours.

Folley wrinkled his nose against the foul coffee. It had likely cooked on the stove since breakfast, the last of the pots made that morning, burning all through the day until now it was just a bitter black liquid. He'd seasoned it amply with whiskey, but the whiskey did nothing to make the coffee more tolerable and neither did the coffee assist the whiskey. Right now, Benton Folley missed Denver. A man could get a decent plate of supper in Denver, and there were pretty gals at the show houses and willing gals at the whore houses. He'd been in Del Norte just less than a month, and it was almost a month too long.

Back in his hotel room, Deputy U.S. Marshal Benton Folley had a warrant for a man named Dicky Cort who was wanted for murder. Three months ago, they got word that Cort was prospecting in the San Juan Mountains west of a place called Del Norte, and Folley's boss sent him here to bring back Cort. The prospectors would be coming down for the winter, and every one of them would come through Del Norte. Or that's what they said, at least. Benton Folley had laid eyes on scores of prospectors over the last three weeks, but he'd not seen one single Dicky Cort. He was ready to give up when he encountered a prospector who said he knew Cort and that he'd seen Cort in a camp about two months back. This man seemed convinced that Dicky would be along shortly, even though the flow of prospectors coming down out of the mountains had all but dried up.

Across the saloon, the bartender held a plate of food into the air and looked at Benton Folley sitting at the table under the oil lamp.

"This is yours," the bartender shouted to him.

Just as the deputy marshal stood up to go and fetch the plate, the door to the saloon swung open. A draft of cold air swept through the place, and several men shouted at the man on the threshold to close the door. Folley glanced that way to see who'd come in, and the man locked eyes with the deputy marshal and then started straight for him.

"Are you that marshal?" the man asked. He was wearing a heavy, wool overcoat and had a thick beard and a fur hat. Folley thought he recognized the man from around town.

"I'm a deputy U.S. marshal."

"You better come with me," the man said.

"Come with you where?" Folley asked. "I was just about to have my supper."

"Well, you better forget that and come with me," the man said.

Now Folley realized where he'd seen the man. It was the hat that threw him off. Under that hat, the man was bald, and the hat disguising the absence of hair had also made the man hard to recognize.

"You're the hostler," Folley said.

"That's right."

"Is there something wrong with my horse?"

"No, sir," the hostler said, agitated. "I need you to come with me to the doc's apartment. A man just come into town, says he needs to speak to the law."

Folley looked at the plate of food left unattended on the bar. It was just beef stew, and if last night's supper and the previous night's supper could be depended upon, the beef would be stringy, the vegetables would be undercooked, and the broth would be too salty by half. But it was more supper than he'd had so far, and he hated to abandon it.

"What's he need to speak to the law about?" Folley

asked.

"He says he's a cavalry sergeant out of Fort Garland, and he says there's a mess of troopers up in the mountains that have been murdered."

Foley's stomach growled at him, but he heaved a heavy sigh and nodded to the hostler.

"Let me get my coat and hat, and then you can take me to the doctor's apartment."

***

Claim jumpers.

Word spread quickly in the town overrun with prospectors. Many of the men still in Del Norte and who planned to winter here had passed by the scene of the massacre on the banks of the Rio Grande. Some who were in Del Norte were part of the party who helped to bury the murdered men. They'd worried over and discussed the likelihood that the Indians responsible for killing those prospectors would still be in the hills come spring. Some had considered giving up on paying gold claims. Some, who had decided the little bit of placer gold they were getting wasn't worth their lives, had already left Del Norte for Santa Fe. But now, word spread quickly of the tale told by the sergeant from Fort Garland, and the word was claim jumpers.

Anyone would have guessed the hostler was responsible for the rapid spread of the gossip, but in fact two men who had spent the last week bedded down in the hayloft were the culprits. The hostler enlisted their help to get the sergeant to the doctor's apartment, three rooms that the doctor rented over a hardware store. Those men were present to hear Sergeant O'Keefe's story. After getting the injured man to the doctor, the two went quickly to a tent saloon that they favored. Seventeen drinkers and card players in the tent saloon listened to what they had to say as they repeated the sergeant's story, and to the great disappointment of the proprietor, the place emptied as soon as the story was done.

So when Benton Folley came down from the doctor's apartment, already a crowd was gathered in the street. It was dark out, but fires burned in barrels on the street corners and the light of lamps shone through windows, and most of the men in the street recognized Folley as the deputy marshal from Denver.

"Is it true that claim jumpers was responsible for that massacre?" some man shouted at him while he was still on the stairs at the side of the building.

Folley already knew what he had to do, though the idea did not originate with him. The injured sergeant had said it.

"It's true," he called out to the crowd, using the stairs outside the doctor's apartment as a kind of stage from which to address the crowd. "They've butchered a cavalry patrol, too. There's an army sergeant, O'Keefe, up in the doctor's apartment who gave me the story. I'm putting together a posse. I need men who know how to use a gun. There's two dozen of them up there, and there's two cavalrymen still alive, or they were three days ago."

"When are you leavin' out, Marshal?" some man asked.

"Right now," Folley said. "I'm taking volunteers and heading out as soon as we're provisioned and supplied."

Christopher Johnston, who had been in the doctor's apartment and also had heard the sergeant's story, was standing above Folley on the stairs. Johnston owned the hardware store. His apartment was in the back of the store, and he'd heard the commotion of the men trying to get the sergeant up the stairs, so he'd come out to lend a hand. In the last eight months, Johnston had sold a thousand shovels and two thousand picks. He'd sold hundreds of cradles – just as fast as he could get them shipped to his store, he sold them. He'd sold countless boots by the pair and enough lanterns and oil to light the night from here to California. He'd earned far more than the average prospector, and the only soul in Del Norte who might have earned more since they'd opened the San Juan Mountains to prospectors was Madame Marie who had the only true brothel in town, though there were plenty of other whores working out of tents and cabins and apartments.

And it was true that Chris Johnston was so tight he squeaked even after he was oiled. But standing on the staircase outside the doctor's apartment, Johnston made a business decision.

He saw the mood of the crowd, and they were not lathered over the massacre of the soldiers. In truth, probably very few of them were particularly bothered by the massacre of the prospectors. It was the reason the prospectors were killed that had this crowd enraged. Any man who toiled in the river for gold wanted to see every claim jumper out there strung up by the neck. The crime of murder hadn't raised their hackles, but the crime of claim jumping.

"I'll provision the posse," Johnston shouted, and a cheer erupted from the men gathered in the street. The thought of the lost revenue sending out guns and ammunition and probably blankets and maybe even a few canvas tents – it turned his stomach. But those prospectors in the street who were ready to ride back into the mountains for vengeance, they would never forget that when claim jumpers massacred good, hard-working prospectors, it was Christopher Johnston, Proprietor of Hard Ware & Dry Goods, who stood beside the decent men seeking to punish these claim jumpers. Every man in that street would forever buy his supplies from Chris Johnston.

A saloon owner, who'd also earned a good living off of these prospectors – and intended to do even better this winter when so many of them were wintering in Del Norte – he was equally moved by Johnston's generosity. The saloon owner wasn't as quick as Johnston to see the upside of it, but he knew the parsimonious Johnston would not be offering to provision the men without some benefit to himself. So the saloon owner stepped up.

"I'll offer ten dollars to any man who brings back to me the trigger finger of any of those bastard claim jumpers!" he shouted.

He'd not heard anyone say that there might be as many as twenty-four trigger fingers – forty-eight if it could not be adequately determined if a man shot with his left hand or his right – and he had no idea the amount of money he was chipping in, but he was caught up in the moment, and the cheer that arose from the prospectors in the street and the slaps on the back had him convinced that he was making a wise investment.

Benton Folley had been a lawman since he was sixteen years old. He'd started as a jailer in a small town in Missouri, and he'd worked all the big cowtowns in Kansas. He'd been a deputy sheriff in Missouri during the war, and that had been a helluva time and place for a lawman to cut his teeth. It left him cynical and dubious about the decency of his fellow man, and not much of what he'd seen in Kansas had assuaged his doubts. He figured if there were seventy men in the street who now appeared to be ready to join the posse, he'd be lucky to leave town in two hours with a dozen. Half of these men were already drunk and would be passed out before the posse was set to leave. Of the other half, a third of those would turn coward and go sit in the saloons and drink, a third of them would start thinking about their wives back home and decide against riding in a posse, and if he was lucky, the other third would ride along.

But he'd take whatever he could get.

DAY FOUR

- 36 -

Elliot Turner watched the light of dawn grow in the night sky above him. He'd spent a night too cold to sleep, only managing to doze here and there. When dawn finally broke, he rubbed down the horse with handfuls of straw and massaged the life back into the horse's shoulders and legs. The process helped to warm his own limbs. As the light grew, it showed that clouds had rolled in overnight. Low and heavy, rolling out across the morning sky, the clouds looked like they would bring snow. Probably before the day was done the snow would start, and from the look of those clouds it might never stop.

He'd gone deep into the woods, hoping to lose the

men who'd followed him, but now he needed to work his way back out to something he recognized. He needed to get back out to that trail that would take him down to the Del Norte road. He led the horse down through a draw. Fresh tracks in the snow showed that the deer had been through here in the night.

Every draw, every dry creek bed, every mountain stream, created a natural trail that would lead eventually down to the Rio Grande. Turner knew this much. He just needed to keep finding the natural trails. Draws were the best. Streams might drop over the side of a cliff, and then he'd have to find a trail to the bottom of the cliff. But a draw would usually be easy to walk and then it would flatten out someplace and usually lead to another draw or at least a slope where he could cut back and forth and make a winding path where none existed.

The important part was to keep moving and find his way back out to the trail or down low enough where he could get to the Del Norte road. Even in the places where the slope was easy enough to ride, he was making his way through a heavily forested area and he could not mount the horse and ride through here. The young lieutenant was eager to find a place where he could ride.

Surely, by now, Sergeant O'Keefe had made it to Del Norte and a posse was formed up. Safety was simply a matter of getting down to the Del Norte road and joining up with the posse.

But Turner was not sure that he wanted safety. His prospects had not changed since he'd made the decision to turn back and buy O'Keefe time to get to Del Norte. Ahead of him he still saw a dismal future, beginning with a court martial.

As he made his way lower, through draws and

switchbacks, the lieutenant wondered if there was any way yet to salvage his reputation. He might go back and attempt to face the men in the Stallings outfit – if not arrest them, at least delay them.

The cold of the night, the misery of it, is what turned the lieutenant's thoughts back to a dark place. He'd sunk into a morass of misery where he saw his present condition as a beginning of what was to come.

For three days now, it seemed, Turner had acted ingloriously. Except when he turned back to make a stand on that cliff face on the first day when he lost his command, the young lieutenant had done nothing but run. First, he'd lost his command, then he'd run like a coward, allowing himself to be chased by a riffraff of claim jumpers, a loose band of men whose allegiance appeared to be solely to the gold they could steal. Hired killers. Turner had allowed Levi Stout to talk him into a course of action that not only humiliated himself but also disgraced his uniform. He wasn't fit to be an officer. Or so he told himself.

He knew that Stout had done what he thought was best, and Turner did not blame the scout. But the two men had different notions of duty. Turner gave his allegiance to the uniform he wore, the flag under which he rode, and nation that flag stood for. Stout's allegiance went to his wife, to himself. They were different men with different values. Now, Turner thought, with no other man's allegiances or values or life to consider, he would do what he believed was his duty. He would not run to Del Norte. If O'Keefe did not make it to the town and if no posse was on its way, justice would have to come some other way. He was not going to ride to Del Norte – not going to flee to Del Norte. Instead, Turner decided, he was going to come down off this mountain into the Rio Grande valley, and he was going to do what he had intended to do from the start. He would make a stand, punish as many of these men as he could with his rifle, and Providence would find justice in the end.

And one way or another, Turner would avoid the future that seemed to be his destiny. He would either return having fought or he would die having tried. But he would not go back like a kicked dog with his tail tucked and throw himself on the mercy of his superiors.

He hoped that Stout would make it out, but probably he was already dead.

- 37 -

When Lou Stallings finally realized that he'd been duped again by the cavalry scout, he sent two men back down to the Del Norte road with a message for his brother.

"You tell him to get all the men together, and once they've dealt with that trooper, all of you ride on into Del Norte. I'll be along as quick as I can be."

The other two men still with him, Kurt Kessner and Ronnie Snider, they were not men that Lou knew well. He'd had only the few necessary interactions with them since putting this outfit together. With two dozen men in the party, Lou didn't make friends with most of them. He'd talked to them, of course. He'd eaten his suppers with them and worked beside them. But especially with these two, there was something about both men he didn't like. Lou Stallings and the other men in the outfit, at least those he knew, they were solid men who could be counted on to do a job, even if the job called for them to do rough things where other men might balk. They were men who did what they had to do.

But Kessner and Snider both were different. They seemed to enjoy the roughest parts of the job. Kessner was a German immigrant, and Snider might have been, too. Snider had no discernible accent, but Kessner certainly had a European accent of some sort. Lou didn't think that Ronald was a German name, but he didn't know or much care where names came from.

They sent their horses back with the others, as well.

Lou had figured out pretty fast that if he didn't see the cavalry scout's body on the rocks below the cliff then the man must have made his way up that natural chimney to the ridge above. So when the others were gone with the horses, Lou, Kessner, and Ronnie Snider all climbed up to the ridge from the slope beside the lake. It was not an easy climb, but they made it with some effort. Up on the ridge, they found the tracks of a lone man and began following the scout.

"He's probably got a thirty-minute head start on us," Lou said. "The last time I know for sure he was in that crevice was about three-quarters of an hour ago."

The three men followed the tracks in the snow down into an evergreen forest. In places, they lost the tracks but soon found them again.

Lou expected the man to try to work back up toward the pass that would take him back the way they came down to the Del Norte road. These cavalrymen, and he was thinking maybe there were only two and not three, had no hope but to make it back to Del Norte and round up a posse. But all through the afternoon, Lou followed tracks that suggested the man was just working his way down the mountain, down toward the valley below.

When the sun was getting low and they knew dusk would be on them soon, it was Kessner who said it was time to stop for the night.

"We'll build shelter and have a fire and not freeze tonight," Kessner said. "I won't spend another night like last night."

Lou argued that they should keep going, but Snider sided with Kessner.

"You can go on if you want, but I'm sleeping beside a fire," Snider barked back.

So they camped for the night down in a hollow where the wind wasn't so bad, and they made up a fire larger than they had to because all three of the men were determined to spend a warm night.

At dawn the three men broke camp and started again to follow the tracks in the snow. There'd been no snowfall the previous day, so the tracks left in the afternoon were still just as visible as they were when they were fresh. But lower down the mountainside the snow had not gathered as bad, and several times the men ran into wide bare spots where there was no snow and they failed to find tracks immediately. It took until mid-morning to find the place where Stout camped the night before. The fire was buried, but he'd left the shelter standing. The old mountain men did this in the late fall and winter, a help to anyone who might come along later, caught out in the snow and in need of shelter. But Lou Stallings suspected the army scout had left the shelter for another reason – the same reason he left tracks for them to find and didn't appear to have made any effort to try to cover them.

"He wants us to follow him," Lou Stallings said.

"Why would he want that?" Kessner asked. "He's got to know we plan to kill him when we catch him."

Lou grunted but didn't say any more about it.

"We're a ways behind him now," Kessner said. "If this was his camp, he's probably two hours ahead of us now."

It was true, they'd wasted time through the previous day and even this morning trying to find where tracks that disappeared reappeared, but it seemed unlikely to Stallings that the man could have extended his jump on them by that much. Stallings tried to move along faster, but with a nagging in the back of his mind. Tommy Irons had said the scout was a man who knew his business, yet he'd left a trail they could follow with only the smallest of difficulty.

"You're better at following tracks than I am," he said to Snider a short while later. "You take the lead and see if you can't close the distance on him."

It only made sense to Lou Stallings that the scout was letting them follow because he intended an ambush. If so, Lou didn't want to be the man out front. So he put Ronnie Snider in the lead and kept his eyes on the horizon while Ronnie watched the ground in front of them.

The tracks continued to lead them lower down the side of the mountain, down draws and switchback trails that led around rock faces. They went along deer paths through evergreen forests and out through snow-covered mountain meadows.

Late in the morning, they found themselves in a

cluster of aspens, some of them specked with a few leaves, most of them brown now, but some among the leaves stubbornly held to their vibrant gold, a small glimpse of what this spot must have looked like just a few weeks before. A clear mountain stream ran along at the edge of the aspens. They followed the tracks to the stream, and there, in a clearing, they could see for the first time how far down the mountainside they'd actually come. Across the valley, two large mountains loomed high above them, giving the first clue that they'd come a long way down. And below them, they could see the valley. Some of it was open, but much of the valley was carpeted in evergreens. When they looked up the way they'd come, the mountain sloped away in such a way that they could not now see the rocky face where the army scout had escaped them the previous morning, nor could they measure the distance traveled.

Lou Stallings cast his gaze over the valley below, squinting into it as if he might see the army scout down among the pines.

"The road isn't down there," he announced. "The Rio Grande doesn't cut through here. It must be in the valley beyond these mountains across from us."

A low saddle between the two mountains across the valley – that was the place where the scout would go. It was the only place where the scout could go. That low saddle would empty them into the far valley and a man could walk to the Rio Grande valley by dark. Depending on where the pass emptied out, a man might even be on the road to Del Norte by dark.

"We've got to catch him before he gets beyond that pass," Lou said.

The three men hurried. Snider walked out in front now, and he set a good, fast pace. It was easy to follow the tracks. The snow was virtually untouched here. Occasionally they would see deer or other animal tracks, but the army scout's tracks were as visible and easy to follow as they could be. So Snider was able to walk quickly. Snider and Kessner both were careless with their rifles. Kessner kept his on a strap over his shoulder. Snider carried his casually in his crossed arms. But Lou Stallings held his rifle ready to shoot, and he allowed the other two men to walk ahead of him several paces. He felt certain as they approached the pass that there was up ahead an ambush waiting, and he did not want to be the first man in line to spring the trap.

"There's a meadow up ahead," Snider called back. "This is the pass, here. It'll take us clear over to the next the valley. It looks like he's already through it."

"Keep moving," Lou said back. "We've got to catch him. Spread out, walk wide across this meadow."

Lou Stallings let the other two men walk on ahead several paces – Kessner to his left and Snider to his right. When both of them were a few yards into the meadow, Stallings stepped off, trailing the other two and following roughly in the footsteps of their prey. The meadow rose to a slight ridge, and that was the point at which they'd go from the north side of these mountains to the south side, and at that crest they should be able to see into the Rio Grande valley, if not have a view of the river itself.

The tracks ahead, though, they looked strange, and Lou Stallings stopped for a moment to try to make sense of what he was seeing. Out in the middle of the meadow, right near the crest of the ridge, the tracks stopped. They went no farther. And just as Stallings started to puzzle out what that could mean, he heard the crack of the rifle.

- 38 -

Levi Stout cut several cedar branches and wove them between two saplings, constructing a wall of cedar branches. From behind the wall, he scooped up snow, and he piled that onto the wall of cedar branches he'd constructed, blending the wall with the snow so that from a distance it all took on a natural appearance. In a short time, he was satisfied with his work.

If a hawk or an owl had perched on a branch nearby, he might have been confounded by the movements of the man in the heavy wool coat. When Stout came upon the saddle between the two mountains and saw the wide clearing and the snow-covered meadow, the man stopped.

For several moments, maybe a full two minutes, he stood without moving his feet, just twisting his body and looking at the terrain in all directions. Then the man walked out into the clearing, and he placed his feet deliberately. Two or three times he stopped in his own tracks and twisted his body, looking back. When he reached a far point along the clearing, he stopped and again twisted so that he could look back the way he'd come, and then the man began scooped up a large armful of snow. He then began to walk backward into the clearing, carefully placing his feet in the tracks he'd just left, and toting with him a mound of snow.

To a hawk or an owl perched on a branch, even a bird that might have studied the behavior of men, the movements might have seemed bizarre, but Levi Stout had read an opportunity in the terrain, and now he was building a plan.

The clouds overhead threatened snow. Before he reached the Rio Grande valley and the road to Del Norte, Stout expected snow to begin falling again. Likely, it would be a heavy snow, and it might be the kind that would last for days. Survival now dictated that he had to consider the possibility that he would not make it to the Del Norte road easily or quickly. It might be that he would have to hole up in a cabin for a day or two, or maybe even a week. He was low on provisions and he might need to hunt.

A fire in a cabin, the sound of a rifle shooting game – if those men were on his trail, Stout would have to believe that they would find him hiding out in a cabin, and there he would be at their mercy.

So he abandoned his hope of outrunning these men and getting to the Del Norte road in front of them. Instead, he was going to war with them. What he had in mind was the sort of thing that some men might balk at – men such as Lieutenant Turner who believed there was honor and glory in war. No, there was only survival. There was only kill or be killed. And Levi Stout intended to survive.

When he'd backed out of the meadow, carefully placing his feet in his own tracks, Stout then walked to the place where he built the wall of cedar branches between the two small saplings. As he went, he carefully placed snow from his armful into his footprints and brushed it so that it blended and looked as if no one had stepped there at all. It was laborious, and cold, but also necessary.

In less than half an hour, Stout had constructed a blind in a place where he had an excellent field of fire. When he was done covering his tracks, he squatted down behind his blind, and there he waited.

Some men might call it murder, what he intended. But Levi Stout did not need philosophy to weigh his intentions, to justify them, or to spare his conscience. In war, there is surviving or not surviving, and Levi Stout intended to survive. Let those others worry about glory and honor, Stout was a man married to a good and willing woman, and he wanted to go home to her.

He waited longer than he expected to, and he'd begun to wonder if there was not pursuit. Maybe the men behind him at the cliff gave up when they discovered he'd escaped. But that seemed unlikely. He waited an hour or so, the cold compounding the while. He occupied himself with watching the gray, rolling clouds above. Those were snow clouds. Any moment the bottom would fall out, and when it did, Stout was certain a big snow would come on. They'd be measuring the snowfall in feet, not inches.

And then he heard voices, muffled so that he could not understand what they said, but unquestionably raised voices.

Stout hardly breathed, not wanting the vapor cloud to

give him away. He'd tried to build the blind so that anyone walking up on it would not notice it, and now was the moment of truth.

He waited, knowing that he would not see them until they had passed the blind. He would strike when they were out in the meadow. He did not know what they might have in the way or numbers or if they would be mounted. He did not think they could be more than five, but they might be fewer. If they were mounted, they could be a problem. He might be able to get two or even three mounted men before they got turned around and charged him.

And then he saw the first of them. The man stopped behind a pine at the edge of the meadow and stood there, watching out through the meadow.

"He could be in those trees out across the way," the front man said, calling back to someone who Stout could not yet see. "The tracks go across the meadow."

The man was in full view, standing at the edge of the meadow. If he turned and looked, he'd see Stout.

The scout nestled himself closer to the ground. He'd packed up a small rim of snow around his blind, and he tried to lower himself into the earth in hopes that the snow would prevent him from being seen. And then a second man walked into view, doubling the chance that one of them would turn and see Stout. There was still at least one man that Stout could not yet see, crunching through the snow as he walked toward the other two.

Stout breathed lightly, almost not at all, and waited. One hand was under him, ready to push him off the ground. The other clutched his rifle. If they turned his direction, he would spring up and fight them as best he could. It would be an even match if it happened, except that there were at least three of them and just the one of him.

A third man now stepped into view, and the three men talked for just a moment, though Stout could no longer hear what they said. The third man had his rifle at the ready, like he was expecting an ambush. The other two were lackadaisical about their weapons, but this third man was ready for a shootout.

They spread out now, the third man letting the other two step forward to his right and left. He waited, allowing them to advance into the meadow a few paces.

Stout let them walk. He wanted them clear out in the meadow. He didn't want them to be in a place where they could easily dash back to the cover of the trees.

Levi Stout raised himself up on one knee and shouldered the rifle. He looked down the barrel, sighting his target. He started to slowly release a breath, his entire focus on the smallest part of back of the head covered by his front sight. He squeezed the trigger.

***

Stout aimed first the farthest man out, the one on the right.

The decision was a choice made in an instant. The one in the center seemed like the bigger threat, but Stout decided to eliminate the one farthest away because he was the one who could be out of range the fastest. The bullet flew true, finding its target, and in an instant, there were only two men standing in the meadow. The one on the left was closest, even though he was a good five yards farther into the meadow. His rifle went to his shoulder and he dropped to a knee. But the shot had come in the distraction of the quiet, and he didn't know in which direction to point his rifle.

Stout swung his rifle now to the man in the center – the one who'd had his rifle ready from the start and had been the last one into the meadow. But the man had been ready, and somehow, he seemed to have already discovered the ruse. He had spun around and was facing back into the trees, searching for the source of the rifle shot. And he found it just about the time Stout put his sights on the man.

The two rifles sprang to life simultaneously. Both shots missed their mark, though Levi Stout heard the snap of the bullet as it flew past and cracked into a tree just beyond him. Another rifle barked, and Stout saw that the man on the left was now in the fight. It was two against him, but Stout still had his original advantage. He'd laid a trap where both men would be exposed out in the middle of the meadow and he would have some cover from the brush and trees around him.

Stout stepped quickly from his blind, working the action on the Winchester to chamber a fresh round as he stood behind the wide trunk of a tall pine. The men in the field both fired off a second shot, both shots penetrating harmlessly into the pine trunk.

Stout swung the rifle to his shoulder and stepped around the side of the tree so that he was half exposed. The center man was running in the opposite direction, and Stout wasn't sure if he was making for the ridge where he might be able to drop to the ground and find cover behind the slope of the meadow or if he was running as far as he could get, into the trees on the opposite side of the meadow. Either way, the man was seconds away from no longer being a target.

But the man on the left appeared to be unaware that the other had abandoned him, and he was bringing up his rifle to try another shot.

Stout twisted slightly, bringing the left-hand man into the center of the iron sights.

Stout knew he had to stay calm. In Stout's view, two things got a man killed in a shooting fight: Bad luck and panic. Some men just fell victim to chance, and when that happened, no man could deny that fate determined a result. In the war, a panicked man was likely to leave his ramrod down the barrel of his musket. A panicked man might expose himself unnecessarily. A panicked man didn't hold his rifle steady. A panicked man was a dead man.

The man out in the meadow made his shot, the crack of the rifle boomed out across the field, the lead ripped a splinter away from pine trunk down near Stout's thigh.

The cavalry scout let the man become a blur beyond the front sight. He focused his eye on the front sight, centering it between the buckhorn sights on the rear. He let out his breath, smooth, and then squeezed the trigger.

The man in the meadow jerked as the shot hit true.

Stout swung back to the right, looking for the man who'd been in the center of the three, the one who'd run toward the forest on the far side of the meadow. He was gone, and Stout had the sense he didn't just run to the tree line.

Stout stood for several minutes, one shoulder leaned against the big pine.

The first man he shot was dead in the meadow, Stout

didn't have any doubt about that. He'd shot him in the back of the head. The second man, though, was making noise, moving in the snow. A wounded man could be more dangerous than a wounded bear, and Levi Stout wasn't in a hurry to walk out into that meadow and get himself shot by a dying man looking to kill the man who killed him.

While he waited, he watched the distant tree line. It was hard to see anything from across the meadow. The rise of the meadow, subtle as it was, prevented him from seeing anything lower than about chest height in the trees beyond, and the distance and the darkness within the forest meant that anyone lurking just inside the trees would have been all but invisible. Still, Stout watched for some time, hoping that maybe he would catch a movement that might give away the position of his adversary. But he saw no movement in the forest, nothing that would indicate the presence of the man.

The mountain cliffs rose steep on either side of the pass. There could be no question where the man fled to while Stout focused his attention on the one of the left. The man who'd been in the center of the three, he had to have gone across the meadow.

The second man that Stout shot was still moving out in the meadow, and at last Stout decided to venture out. He took a few tentative steps out into the meadow, abandoning the safety of his pine trunk. Stout kept his eyes moving across the far tree line and then back to the wounded man. The man might be wounded, but he was conscious and capable of moving, and so Stout stayed cautious. The scout knew that a wounded man might sit up with a rifle in hand and get off a shot before Stout could move out of the way, so his eyes moved often and quickly back to the man.

No shot came from the far trees as Stout continued to

walk slowly out into the meadow.

After a few short minutes, Stout was far enough into the meadow to get a good look at the wounded man. It was a gut shot that had struck him. The man was likely killed, and his final hours – whether they were few or stretched into days – would be terribly painful.

"Stallings!" the man shouted, twisting his body to look toward the far tree line where the other man had made his escape.

"I don't think he's coming back for you," Stout said.

The man on the ground hadn't seen him coming, and he winced now, clenching his teeth against the pain, as he lifted his head to look toward Stout.

The man bit back the pain. Every bit of it showed on his face. Stout continued to approach him and he saw that the man's wound was a bit lower than he first thought, down on his hip. The bullet had shattered the hip bone. The effect would be the same. Stout had seen similar wounds in the past – a shattered hip bone, a ricocheted bullet and bone fragments cutting through the man's abdomen. The man's rifle was on the ground beyond his reach, as were his haversack and canteen.

"What's your name?" Stout asked.

"Kurt Kessner."

He had a bit of an accent, and Stout picked him out as a German immigrant.

"You a veteran?"

"I fought in the War Between the States," Kessner said.

"So you know your condition," Stout said.

Kessner looked down at the blood soaking through his trousers and shirt. The wound was on the left side of his body, but the blood had soaked through so that almost the entirety of the top of his trousers and the bottom of his shirt were dark and damp. He clenched his teeth again has he pulled his trousers out from his body to see the wound. He nodded and let go of the trousers.

"You have morphine?" Kessner asked.

"I don't," Stout said.

Kessner grunted and closed his eyes, allowing his bare head to fall back into the snow. He pushed himself with his right leg, turning so that he could better see toward the far trees.

"Did you shoot Stallings, too?" Kessner asked.

"I shot the man out on the far right."

"That was Snider," Kessner said. He drew a sharp, gasping breath. "Stallings will be halfway to Del Norte by now."

Stout chuckled.

"Bit of a coward, is he?" Stout said, his eyes scanning the far tree line. This man dying on the ground was no threat, but the other one might still be.

"Let's just say he'll come out of this alive," Kessner said.

"Which Stallings is it, Jacob or Lou?"

Kessner bit off a laugh.

"Lou. Jacob wouldn't even be out here."

Stout nodded. "I'm going after him. When I get back, I'll send someone for you."

"I'll be dead by then," Kessner said, and Stout watched as the man slid a small, two-shot pocket pistol from his belt. It was tucked behind the scabbard that held his knife.

Stout watched the hand that held the pistol, but Kessner didn't make any movement that suggested he intended to use it.

"Sorry," Stout said feebly, not because he was truly sorry but because he felt he should offer the man something in his final moments.

Kessner, though, dismissed the apology with a scoff. "I'd have done the same to you if I'd had the chance. It's how it goes for men like us. Good luck getting Stallings."

Stout nodded, and now he set off through the meadow, passing Kessner with a wide berth just in case he decided to take a shot with that pistol.

As Stout neared the tree line, following the tracks that Stallings left in the snow and keeping his eyes on the woods for any movement, he heard the sharp crack of a small caliber pistol. He didn't need to glance back. Kurt Kessner did for himself.

The snow that had threatened since dawn now began to fall.

- 39 -

Lieutenant Elliot Turner looked over the edge of the rocky cliff face. The rocky cliff face dropped about forty feet down to a few low, rolling hills. Beyond the hills, he could see the road to Del Norte and the crystal-clear river winding its way through the valley.

The snow had started now, and the gray day was turning white. Big flakes blew in the wind, landing cold on his cheeks. He did not know how far along the road he was, but he knew he was east of the trail he and Stout had taken to get up the mountain. Probably the men who'd chased him were still west of him. If he could find a path down off this cliff and into the valley, he could ride east and make it to Del Norte.

"I don't know which way is right," Turner admitted to the horse, for there was no one else to hear his confession.

Turner had made up his mind. In truth, he'd determined his own fate at least twice. He'd decided to sacrifice himself first when he left Stout and O'Keefe and turned back to ambush the Stallings outfit and again, by morning. But he found himself still nagged by indecision. His good judgment told him that he should make for Del Norte, but that way led to professional ruin, court martial, and disgrace. If he went west, back to face the men who'd murdered his command, there might be some redemption of his reputation, even if it was posthumous.

"There won't be a decision to be made if we don't get down off of this cliff, first," Turner said to the horse, and he took up the lead rope and started moving again.

It was midday now, sometime shortly after noon. Turner had a watch, but somewhere along the way it had stopped working. The gray clouds and the falling snow prevented him from judging the time based on the position of the sun. But he reckoned he'd been making his way along deer paths and through gently rolling meadows for at least five hours, which would put it shortly after noon, probably.

He kept along the edge of the cliff until the slope down eased some and the trees again grew up along the slope, and there he managed to find a path that would get him to the hills below. And there, at last, Turner slid a foot into the stirrup and swung himself up into the saddle. He tugged slightly with his right hand, looking through the falling snow off to the west, and the horse turned to follow his gaze. He'd made his decision, and it was the decision he'd known he would make.

By the time Lieutenant Turner reached the Del Norte road, the snow had gathered in a fresh, undisturbed blanket, but the path of the road was easy enough to make out. One season of prospectors coming and going had been sufficient to wear down the path.

The valley here gave a sense of wide open spaces – the low hills seemed to push back the prominence of the high mountain peaks, and the forests on either side of the river were less forests and more patches of trees. But Turner found with the wind blowing the snow into his face, he had only a limited ability to see any distance. The flakes were large and falling steadily, and the clouds were low, lower than the alpine tundra he'd ridden across the day before.

As he continued the ride west, the mountain walls began to close in, creating a tighter canyon. And then the forests along the banks grew thicker, and the white road ran near the rocky riverbanks with the trees close.

Turner could not say how far he'd ridden. The landscape changed, but the constant falling snow and the thick, gray sky seemed to contain the entirety of the world and all of time, and distance stopped meaning anything.

And then the lieutenant began to recognize parts of the landscape, changed though it was in the steady falling veil. Off to the right, that was where the ambush of the prospectors happened. Turner saw it now, though not in the same way Stout had seen it. The cavalry scout saw the tracks, saw where men had hidden on the hillside, where they had charged, where they had hidden their horses, where they had killed. He saw the tracks that proved what had happened. But the lieutenant saw it in a different way. He saw it in the lay of the land. The winding approach of the road to the hillside would have left the prospectors blind even to the possibility of danger. And the cover on the hillside, the prospectors never could have seen the men hidden on the hillside, or the horses. It wasn't just that the hillside was a good place for an ambush – it was the perfect place for an ambush.

And that's what Turner now saw in the way that he saw things, and he began to realize that as an officer, he needed to see things in his own way, and he needed men like Stout or like the Black Seminoles who scouted for the army, or the Pawnee scouts – he needed them to see the details in the way they saw them. They were all parts of one whole.

Turner knew he had to be somewhere near the place where he and Stout had taken the trail into the mountains, and he expected that's where he would find whatever was left of the Stallings outfit. He urged the horse on a bit faster. He wasn't eager for the fight, but he was eager to see this thing come to an end. The horse obliged, loping out over the snow-covered road, riding back to the west to where he knew he would find a trail cutting north into the mountains and where he hoped he would find the remainder of the Stallings outfit.

***

The snow and the low clouds and the darkness of the gray day hid the smoke from the campfire, and Turner realized he was fortunate to have heard the men when he did. Had he not, he might have ridden right into their camp.

He wheeled the horse when he heard one man shout to another in the echo of the valley and galloped hard to a stand of cedars where he would be hidden from sight.

There, he dropped down out of the saddle and drew his Winchester rifle from its scabbard. He tied off the horse behind the trees and in a crouch worked over to the edge of the branches. Looking through the raining snow, Turner now saw them. In a stand of trees on the opposite side of the river, two men who appeared to be collecting firewood. They were separated by probably thirty yards or more and were still shouting to each other. Turner believed they had not seen him. He could clearly see one of the men, within a stand of aspens, still holding a bundle of sticks and branches in his arms. The other was not clear to him, just a shadow in the woods, but that man also made no movement that would suggest he was alert to the presence of the cavalry officer.

Turner held his position and watched the two men for several minutes as they finished collecting their firewood and then disappeared deeper into the forest.

Now he quickly untied the horse and started off back down the road, keeping an eye across the river at the trees and watching for any sign of the men.

He would have to cross the river, though that would not be a problem. The Rio Grande here ran wide and shallow, and when Turner had ridden down past a bend in the river, he tugged the reins. The horse balked at first but then willingly took a step into the river. Sure-footed, the gelding crossed without ever getting his knees wet. Up on the opposite bank, Turner dismounted and led the horse back behind a bluff. He kicked away a good patch of snow to reveal patches of grass, and left the horse to graze, picketed there.

Rifle in hand, Turner picked his way among the tall pines and thick cedar and fir. He could smell the smoke of the campfire, though he could not see their camp through the trees and snow.

He dropped down into a ravine and walked that some distance, following the smell of the smoke, and then using a cedar tree for cover, he emerged out the other side, and there about thirty yards away he saw the camp. A dozen horses or more were tied inside a ring of big pines, and several canvas tents stood near the horses with a quantity of snow collecting on the sides. By the tents, Turner saw the campfire. It was burning strong with the flames licking high, and three men stood by the fire. One of them had his arm bandaged and a bandage wrapped around his head.

Turner went prone at the lip of the ravine, burrowing into the snow and pushing it away from his body until he was mostly against bare rock, with a fair amount of snow in front of him to help hide his presence.

The men were indifferent to all around them. As he watched, Turner realized there was a fourth man by the fire, lying under blankets.

These were the injured, he realized – men left behind by the others, and Turner reasoned they probably were left to bury their dead and tend to their own wounds and keep the horses.

At least one of them looked like he had no injuries, but the other two standing by the fire, they appeared to be nursing fresh injuries. The one had bandages wrapped on his head and arm, and the other walked with a limp. Turner tried to think of how these men might have picked up their wounds, and all he could figure was that they were in the midnight melee with Stout below the cliff when Turner had gone back to try to ambush the men.

Their injuries did nothing to draw out any sympathy in the young lieutenant. He saw them, and his blood boiled with hatred. These were men who were part of the dawn charge on his men. These were men who had snuck up on his encampment and surprised his troopers. These were men who were responsible for the loss of his career, the loss of his future.

Was it justice or vengeance that made Turner raise up the Winchester and look down the sights at one of the men? He did not know for sure, nor did he much care.

The moment he squeezed the trigger, he would have both.

- 40 -

The five men were riding along the Del Norte road, still in sight of the mountain trail they'd ridden down, when they heard the shooting.

Dicky Cort cocked his head at the first shot and twisted in his saddle, looking back at Jacob Stallings.

"That was a shot," Dicky said.

Jacob, Dicky, and Texas Eddie spent a comfortable night in an abandoned cabin they'd come across, building up a good campfire. Dicky Cort even found a cot to sleep on. The other two men who came behind them, driving the horses, smelled the smoke from their campfire and joined them in the cabin. So all five men were well rested and feeling much improved over the previous morning, though Texas Eddie woke with a head full of congestion.

They spent some time in the morning trying to find tracks to pick up the trail of the cavalryman, but their efforts were unsuccessful. Seeing the dark clouds that threatened snow, Jacob Stallings made the decision that they would go below and deal with Lou's anger later. None of them wanted to be hanged, but all of them had just about resigned themselves to the prospect of changing their names and leaving Colorado Territory for good. Jacob Stallings still held to some notion that he could file a claim and sell it and then skedaddle, but he hadn't worked out yet how he would accomplish that.

They'd just come down off the trail and were looking for the rest of their party when they heard the rifle boom, its deep echo muffled some by the falling snow.

A moment later, before anyone could answer Dicky, they heard another shot.

"Where's it coming from?" Jacob Stallings asked. He had a sudden excitement as he thought that almost surely it was the man they'd been chasing.

"It's coming from across the river," Dicky said. "Could be a mile down yonder."

Now the five men left the spare horses and rode toward the river, looking for a place to cross. But they did not need a ford, for the river bed here was wide and the water ran shallow enough that it was easy to simply walk the horses across. The few deep channels that might have plunged the horses into water up to their bellies were easy enough to see and narrow enough to avoid.

Up on the other bank, the five men moved forward

cautiously. There'd been several more shots as they crossed the river. Clearly someone was exchanging shots with someone else.

Through a gap in the trees, Texas Eddie saw a horse picketed in a clear patch.

"Look there!" Eddie said.

"We're on foot from here," Dicky Cort said, swinging out of the saddle and drawing his rifle. Dicky knew that this wasn't Jacob's specialty and someone else had to take charge now.

Another crack of a rifle, and this one near enough that all of the men ducked their heads.

"Where's it coming from?" Jacob asked, narrowing his eyes and scanning the woods in front of them.

"He's going to be in there somewhere," Dicky said. "Come on now, and spread out."

The five men all instinctively walked in a crouched position, each one of them about five yards from the man on his left shoulder, and they walked slowly, picking out their steps carefully, scanning the woods all around for any sign of the shooters they'd heard.

They heard one more shot, a lone shot that came after the initial cluster of shooting, but then the shooting seemed to be over. Someone had won the battle.

Dicky Cort found the tracks in the snow at the edge of the ravine, and in a hushed voice he called the others over to him. They did not drop down into the ravine, but they followed the tracks down in the ravine from the bank until they could see a place on the opposite side where the snow had been cleared away. For all the world, it looked like someone had pushed the snow away and used the edge of the ravine there as cover from which to shoot behind.

And then Dicky held up a hand to stop everyone else. He smelled the campfire. Without saying a word, Dicky dropped down into the ravine and positioned himself in the space that was cleared away. Dicky noticed the spent shells nestled in the snow around him, he saw six right away, and then he saw another. This is where one of the shooters had been, no question about it. And now he saw it – their tents, their picketed horses, their campfire. This was the remainder of the Stallings outfit, the men left behind to bury the dead and tend to their wounds. But where there should have been four men, Dicky saw only one, a cavalry officer kneeling down by the fire.

If he'd had a clear shot, Dicky would have taken it right there and then. But the cavalryman was half hidden behind a tree, and was squatting down so low that Dicky just couldn't get an aim on him.

"He's over there," Dicky said, twisting around and calling softly to the others. He motioned with his hand and nodded with his head, urging them to see the army man.

Jacob Stallings craned his neck and stood on his toes, and then he saw the campfire and the tents.

"Shoot him!" Jacob whispered at Dicky.

Dicky turned and looked at the cavalryman, but the man hadn't moved and Dicky still did not have a clear shot. He couldn't so much see what the man was doing as he recognized a familiar movement in the man's body, and Dicky knew that the cavalryman was reloading his rifle.

Texas Eddie had endured enough of this.

He felt miserable. He had a bad cough that he was trying to hold back for fear of alerting the cavalryman and his head ached with all the snot filling it up. And he believed that if he waited for these two to make a decision and deal with the army officer, they'd be waiting here all day. Texas Eddie wanted to get over there and warm himself by that fire and lay down under one of those tents. So he dropped down into the ravine and scrambled up the other side, past Dicky Cort who was still lying prone on the rock where the snow had been covered away.

Eddie came up the other side of the ravine without any effort at concealing himself or his movements. If they'd been hunting game, they'd have lost it right there and then.

And right then, the game they were hunting spotted Texas Eddie.

The cavalryman rose up, bringing his carbine to his shoulder. Texas Eddie was faster, squeezing off a round from the hip that tore through the canopy of the trees and missed its mark by a dozen feet.

But Dicky Cort had already brought up his rifle when Eddie started through the ravine, and he'd taken aim right on the spot where the cavalryman now stood.

Dicky fired a round that knocked the cavalryman to the ground, and Texas Eddie started forward at a run, his rifle now at his shoulder and his finger on the trigger.

- 41 -

Turner aimed his Winchester carbine at the man coming through the snow toward him, but the shot came from somewhere else. Turner never saw it. The shot hit him like a hammer and fell back, sprawled on the ground in the snow. At first, he didn't know what hit him. But in a moment that seemed like an eternity, Turner connected the sound of the rifle to the impact that knocked him down.

There'd been two rifle shots, he realized. He saw the man charging him first a shot from the hip that ripped high overhead, but he'd only heard the other shot.

There'd been a punch to his chest that laid him flat on

his back, but he felt no pain now. He still had his wits, and he'd had the presence of mind to hold his rifle as he went down. Now he tried to raise himself up, but he felt a tremendous weight that held him back. He looked down the length of his body and saw that the man charging at him through the snow was still coming. He was almost to the fire pit, and his rifle was at his shoulder.

Turner stopped trying to sit up. He raised his rifle and squeezed off another shot, one-handed like he was holding a pistol. The rifle bounced in his hand, but through the puff of white gunsmoke and the dark gray stream of smoke rising up from the campfire and the big, white flakes pouring down through the canopy of the trees, Turner saw the man suddenly release his own gun, both hands going for his neck. Then he saw the blood running between the man's fingers, running out from under his hands. The flow of blood suggested that he'd not only shot the man in the neck, but he'd hit an artery. It was so much blood leaking from the man's throat.

Turner watched as the man's eyes grew wide and his face went pale, and the young lieutenant could see in the man's face a realization that death was on him. Briefly, in just the instant that it takes for thoughts to form, Turner wondered what it was like for the man to know that this was it, that this was the end – or even if he did. Instead, did the man think he needed to get a friend who could patch him up? Did he think if he squeezed shut the wound he could staunch the blood?

But then the thoughts were past, the man slipped to the ground and away from where Turner could see him, and the lieutenant now tried to get up again. At least one more man was still in the woods somewhere, and Turner needed to get up and deal with that man.

The weight, though.

The lieutenant couldn't reason through it. He reached up to his chest to try to push away whatever it was that held him down, but there was nothing there. He'd taken off his gloves to reload his rifle and had not yet put them back on when the fresh round of shooting started, and now his bare hand fell upon something warm and moist. He held his hand up where he could see it, and realized it was covered in blood.

He was shot. There was no weight on him. He'd been shot in the chest and the injury, whatever it was, had made it impossible for him to lift himself. And now, with the realization, came the pain. It was not waves of pain, but a constant, steadily growing thing. It was mostly under his left shoulder.

Turner rolled onto his right side, keeping his rifle clutched in his hand, and he scooched himself along on the ground on his elbow and knee. He kept his rifle clenched in his fist.

He heard the rifle thunder behind him and heard the bullet smash into a tree not far from where he was. He was not sure where he was going. He just knew that he needed to get himself behind cover and try to get his rifle up so that he could protect himself.

Beyond the tents there was a large pine that had fallen some time ago. It was rotting and the bark had mostly come away from it. The big tree trunk made up a kind of perimeter for the campsite. Turner got to the tree and steeled his strength to fling himself up and over the tree. What should have been a simple thing turned out to be a terrible strain, but he managed it, managed to get himself propped up on the pine trunk and then roll off onto the other side. As he did it, a couple of bullets smashed into the trunk near him, but they did not find their target.

Still, whoever was back at the ravine, whether it was one man or a dozen, they knew now that he was hurt. They'd seen him try to fling his body up and over that tree trunk, and even if they failed to see the wet blood on his coat, they had to see how he struggled just to crawl over the pine tree.

Turner felt the struggle in his chest to get a breath. Had the bullet punctured a lung? Had it broken a rib? He didn't know, and he could get much of a look at his chest to determine. Every movement was a strain. There was pain, certainly. But worse than the pain was the fatigue that seemed to have swept over him. He felt weak in an unnatural way. But he knew he had to push through the weakness. He propped himself up against the pine tree, sitting on his hip, and he lifted the carbine up to rest on the tree, pointing back toward the ravine.

His left arm was useless. He had to prop the gun against the felled trunk and manipulate the rifle with just his right arm.

Three men appeared out of the ravine, and then a fourth. All four men had rifles up, and they were scanning the woods. They might have seen him go over the tree, but they clearly did not see him now.

Turner sighted down the barrel of the Winchester. He'd been rated a marksman back at West Point. He squeezed the trigger and the bullet smashed into the face of one of the men near the ravine. It was definitely a kill shot. The man's entire face seemed to erupt into a cloud of pink mist and the man fell back into the ravine.

"Dicky!" one of the others shouted, and that man turned and jumped back into the ravine, apparently to help the other.

Turner's shot had found its mark, but he'd also given

away his position. The two others now opened fire on the pine trunk, and lead chewed into the rotten wood. Turner dropped his head low and just tried to wait it out. With his one functioning arm, he worked the action on the carbine to eject the spent casing and chamber a fresh round. The young lieutenant tried to keep himself calm, though the pain in his chest and a growing fear of the wound made it difficult to stay calm.

The explosion of gunfire from the two men now ceased, but Turner found his ears were ringing from so many shots being fired.

He twisted a little, picking his head up just enough to look down the barrel of the gun. The two men were both now reloading, and they'd not even taken the precaution of getting behind cover. Did they think they'd hit him? Turner squeezed the trigger. For a moment, Turner didn't understand what happened. Then he realized his shot had hit the other man's rifle, knocking it from his grasp. Quickly, the lieutenant stretched his fingers to work the lever on the carbine, he didn't want to miss the chance to get another shot off. Almost without taking time to aim, he fired another shot, and this one struck its target, hitting the man in the side and spinning him around. Again, Turner stretched his fingers to work the lever. He brought it up and found his target in the sights and fired a third time. This shot struck the man in the chest.

The other one now had loaded his rifle and was returning fire. A shot struck the pine trunk and ricocheted – or maybe broke free a splinter. Either way, something bounced up from the tree trunk and struck Turner in the side of the head, knocking his hat askew and creasing his scalp.

"Ah!" Turner shouted. The cut across his head hurt worse than the wound to his chest, though he knew the latter was far more serious. The man fired another shot, and then another. Both of them cut into the tree trunk, and Turner thought that soon there would not be much less other than a wet mush of rotten tree flesh.

Now Turner shifted the Winchester carbine and he let loose another shot. He aimed low, not on purpose, and hit the man in the thigh. The man fell to one knee. Now they both worked the levers on their rifles. It seemed a race, which man could chamber a round, aim, and shoot faster than the other.

The lieutenant won the race. Though he was adjusting the rifle with just one good arm, Turner managed to get the faster aim. This time it was a gut shot, and the man fell back and dropped down into the ravine.

There remained at least one man over there, the one who'd gone into the ravine after one of the men Turner had shot. That one who jumped into the ravine, he hadn't been wounded in the shooting.

Turner stayed where he was for several minutes, his rifle trained on the ravine. Blood was running down his cheek from the wound to his head. He could feel it, but he did not dare take his hand off his rifle to wipe it away. He realized that his breathing was becoming even more labored.

It seemed early for night to be falling, but a darkness was creeping in all around the lieutenant.

Still, no one appeared from out of the ravine. Was the man just waiting?

The snow was beautiful coming down through the forest, and Elliot Turner didn't really even feel the cold any more. He didn't feel much of anything, except very tired. There was an ache, to be sure, in his chest. If he really focused, he could feel the throbbing of his head under his hat band.

At length, the lieutenant rolled over onto his back. Above him, the canopy of the trees opened up like the end of a long tunnel, and beyond he could see the gray sky. It didn't seem so dark now, looking up at it, and Turner wondered why it was he'd thought night was falling. He felt very comfortable, the snow like a soft bed below him. The flakes that hit his face were cold, but it was pleasant to feel them.

He'd avenged his command. He found those four men in the campsite and he lit into them. He'd killed them, even walking over to the wounded man who was unarmed and putting a bullet in that man's face when the other three were dead. Then he'd killed four of these men who came up behind him. Maybe he hadn't killed all four of them, but he'd shot four of them. The one he shot in the throat was surely dead, as was the one he'd shot in the face. The other two would probably die of their wounds.

One of them was left alive, but Turner felt he'd done what he came to do. Maybe it was vengeance for his lost command, the men of his patrol. Maybe it was redemption for his lost honor. He'd stayed behind and fought, and he'd punished these murderers.

Maybe it was both, vengeance and redemption, and maybe it was justice, too.

Turner could hear the campfire just beyond the fallen pine tree. It crackled and spit and sounded warm. He felt mesmerized by the snow falling free through the open canopy of the trees.

- 42 -

The Rio Grande valley had to lie beyond the pass. Lou Stallings knew this. And the road to Del Norte, it had to be there in the valley. Nevertheless, when Stallings came out of the forest into the meadow and saw the wide river, he felt a sense of relief as if a miracle had just lighted on him.

He'd walked so far, and the cold and the snow did not quit.

He'd fallen.

Watching his backtrail and hiking through snow that was rapidly piling up, he'd missed a branch under the snow and it got tangled up in his feet, and he went over. A stupid thing. But he'd landed hard on his arm, and now it ached.

Lou Stallings wasn't the sort of man to whine at hardship, but he felt weary and beaten. If that army scout showed up behind him right now, Lou might just be willing to throw down his arms and surrender. He'd lost any hope of a payout. He half expected this thing to end with a noose around his neck.

He hit the Del Norte road, though, and felt a burst of hope. He headed east. He saw no landmarks that looked familiar to him, but he moved as fast as he could. He knew he left tracks in the snow, but it would be a waste of time to try to hide his tracks in any way, and possibly dangerous. He didn't trust his boots to walk through the river without freezing his feet, and that was the only thing he could think of to do that would hide his tracks. But the army scout would know he'd gone east. Of course he would go east. So he just left tracks in the snow. Maybe he'd get somewhere and try to get a shot off at the man. Maybe he'd lead that army scout right into the bosom of his outfit and then they'd have him.

All Lou Stallings knew for sure was that he had to keep putting one foot in front of the other.

He followed the river down through a canyon with high rock walls on either bank. The forests closed in on him and then fell away, spreading out and giving way to open hillsides. Lou figured he'd gone probably six miles or more along the road when at last he started to recognize some of the landmarks. A peak that looked familiar to him. A bend in the river that he seemed to remember. It all looked a little different, covered in snow, but he thought he must be getting close to where they'd left the road to follow the cavalrymen up the mountain trail two days before.

And then he came upon the place where they'd attacked the cavalry patrol at dawn. He did not walk into the woods to see the place, but through the trees from the road, Stallings could see the body of one of the troopers, now half covered in snow.

And then he came to the valley meadow down below, that's where most of the cavalry horses had congregated. Stallings would have been grateful to see one of them now, but the horses were all gone, probably they'd gone back toward Del Norte. Horses were funny about that. They'd find their way home. It wouldn't surprise him if most of those horses made it all the way back to Fort Garland.

As he came out through the meadow, Stallings heard what sounded like shooting. It was far off, nothing that threatened him, but probably something he should worry about. If there'd been anywhere else to go, Lou Stallings might have turned around and headed off in another direction. But there wasn't anything else for it. He just had to keep putting one foot in front of the other, and he would deal with whatever was waiting for him up ahead when he got there.

He took a moment to give his legs a rest. He didn't sit. There was nowhere not covered in snow where he could sit. But he turned and watched his backtrail out across the meadow. The snow was flat and pretty and undisturbed, except where he'd cut his path. There the snow was broken and gray or brown where the mud from his steps mixed with it.

He saw no sign of the cavalry scout, so he started moving again.

***

Night was coming on when Lou Stallings smelled the smoke of a campfire. Because it was dark, he was able to see the glow from the forest across the river, and he decided to take a chance that the rest of his outfit was over there. Stepping lightly in the water, Stallings crossed the river and then walked cautiously through the woods. He heard a horse nicker, and through the trees now he saw the horses picketed, the tents standing. He took a step and saw someone jump up near the campfire, a rifle coming up.

Lou Stallings dropped his head under his arms and ducked behind a tree just as the man in the camp fired off a shot from the rifle.

"Hey!" Lou shouted. "Stop that! It's me."

Now he poked his head around the tree and saw his brother standing there.

"Don't shoot me, Jake."

Jacob Stallings looked pale like he might be sick, and he threw the rifle onto the ground.

"Lou," he said, and he came forward through the camp and threw his arms around his brother, an embrace that was so uncommon that Lou Stallings could not remember having ever hugged his brother before.

"What the hell?" Lou asked.

"They're all dead," Jacob said, and Lou realized that his younger brother was in a bad state, deeply disturbed.

"Who's all dead?" Lou said.

"The entire outfit. Everybody."

Jacob Stallings nodded his head to Texas Eddie, whose body he'd dragged away from the camp and left with the others. There were seven bodies there, all men who were part of their outfit, all men who Lou Stallings recognized. The older man let out a string of curses under his breath.

"What about Dicky?" Lou said.

"He's in that ravine over there," Jacob said.

"Tell me what happened," Lou said.

So Jacob told him – told him about hearing the shooting as they came up on the camp and finding the cavalry officer in the camp and the four men they'd left behind all dead.

"Eddie went after him," Jacob said. "He charged him. But he shot Eddie. Then he shot Dicky – shot Dicky right in the head. And I jumped down into the ravine to try to take care of Dicky, but he was killed. And then that cavalryman, he killed the other two. And it was just me, down in the ravine."

"Where's he at now?" Lou asked.

"Hell, I don't know," Jacob said. "I stayed down in the ravine until he was gone."

As they talked, Lou made his way over to the campfire to warm himself. Jacob moved with him so that the two of them continued their conversation with the smoke from the campfire blowing around them.

"What about Kessner and Snider?" Jacob asked.

"Dead," Lou Stallings said. "The scout managed to get off the cliff and then he ambushed us."

Jacob started to say something, to criticize his brother as was his nature, but then he stopped himself. The realization that all their carefully laid plans had come unraveled was a significant blow to the younger man's ego. That they'd lost all their men – the entirety of the twenty-two men they'd hired on killed over the last four days – was devastating.

"What do we do?" Jacob asked.

"We know that three troopers got away from our attack the other morning," Lou said. "I've been thinking about it. There ain't but the two up here. The one you chased yesterday on horseback, and the one I chased on foot. The third one has gone on to Del Norte."

Jacob gave his brother a severe look. "You think so?"

"Has to be," Lou said. "Which means they've already formed up a posse in Del Norte, and like as not they know our names by now."

"How would they know our names?" Jacob asked.

"I'm guessing Tommy Irons told them. What happened to him? I expect Tommy saw that this thing was going to get away from us and he hightailed it to Del Norte to rat us out."

Jacob felt sick in his stomach.

"Our only hope now is to just abandon all of this and get out of this territory as fast as we can. We can get down to Santa Fe and maybe head into Arizona Territory. Nobody will come looking for us there."

"What about the other two?" Jacob asked. "The scout and the other trooper?"

Lou looked up through the canopy at the sky. It was getting dark, now. Night would be on them soon. Despite the fire, Lou was cold and hungry and needed to sleep.

"The tents are set up, the fire is burning," Lou said. "We'll camp here tonight. In the morning, we'll ride out of here. Make for Del Norte as fast as we can, but we'll ride in at night when no one will see us and sniff out what they know or don't know. And from there, we'll make our way south. We can drive these horses into the town and maybe sell them in Del Norte or somewhere else."

"What about the claim?" Jacob said.

"That's done," Lou said. "That whole thing is finished. We're going to forget about that claim."

"It's a rich claim," Jacob said.

"You can't spend any gold when you're swinging from a scaffolding."

"And what if there is a posse coming from town? We'll meet them between here and there."

"We'll try to avoid them," Lou said.

The brothers stood silently beside the fire, both of them feeling its warmth. Lou tossed another couple of branches from the wood pile onto the fire to keep it blazing.

The fire crackled and a pine branch full of sap popped like a low caliber gun, and both men started at the noise.

Lou Stallings started to chuckle at himself, and Jacob looked up at his older brother and started to chuckle, too. And that's when Lou cast his eyes toward a movement at the edge of the camp, and he stopped laughing when he saw the army scout standing at the edge of the camp with a rifle aimed at a spot right between the two brothers.

- 43 -

"I followed your tracks in," Levi Stout said.

The snow was still falling, and the gray day had turned dark with the onset of dusk, and the army scout looked more like a black shadow than a man standing at the edge of the trees. In fact, Jacob Stallings thought that the man looked more like death than anything else.

"I'm guessing you're Jacob Stallings," Stout said, his eyes fixed on the younger brother. "The two of you look like brothers, and I know you're Lou."

Neither of the Stallings brothers responded. Jacob's eyes dropped to the front of the canvas tent where he'd set his rifle. It was two steps away. Lou Stallings had a six-shooter in a holster on his belt, hidden by his coat.

"You want to go for that rifle?" Stout said to Jacob Stallings. "It wouldn't bother me none if you want to try for it."

"I'm not a fool," Jacob Stallings said, eyeing the rifle in Stout's hand.

"I could make an argument that you are," Stout said. His tone was level and cold, the features of his face were indistinguishable in the growing darkness.

"Are you going to kill us?" Lou Stallings asked.

Stout ignored the question. He nodded his head toward the ravine where Jacob had dragged Texas Eddie and the six other bodies.

"Coming in, I seen a dead man in the ravine, and that pile of dead over there," Stout said. "Where's the man who did all that damage?"

"Gone off," Jacob said.

"Which direction?" Stout asked.

Jacob Stallings flung his head to indicate behind him. "Off that way, I reckon. I was down in the ravine."

"Hiding?" Stout asked.

"I was down in the ravine," Jacob Stallings repeated.

Lou Stallings took a heavy breath and crossed his arms in front of himself. He was trying to get a hand closer to the grip of the pistol on his belt.

"What state was he in when he went off that way?" Stout asked.

"How do you mean?" Jacob asked.

"Was he injured?"

"I thought Eddie or Dicky had shot him, one of them. But I couldn't say for sure. Maybe injured, maybe not."

Stout pursed his lips.

"Where's the rest of your outfit?" Stout asked.

"We're all that's left," Jacob said.

Lou could have knocked his brother in the head for saying it. There was no reason to tell this man anything more.

"I suppose you're planning to take us to Del Norte," Lou Stallings said.

"We'll see how this goes," Stout said.

Lou Stallings grinned and nodded his head.

"You won't get any trouble from us," he said.

Stout nodded once, but he also narrowed his eyes and frowned, and Lou Stallings did not think the cavalry scout believed him.

"We brought two dozen men up for this job," Lou Stallings said. "Some of those men were good friends to me. Phil Wells, Dicky Cort, even Tommy Irons. But you've killed them all."

"Tommy Irons is dead?" Stout asked.

Lou shrugged. "I can't say that for sure. He disappeared a couple of days ago. We ain't for sure what happened to him. But the rest of them are all dead. I suppose you sent a man ahead to Del Norte."

Stout grunted and affirmative response.

"My guess would be that a posse will be here in the morning."

Lou Stallings took a step toward Jacob, and the step positioned him so that he was turned half away from Stout. It seemed an odd choice for a man who was about to go for a pocket gun or a holstered six-shooter, and Stout furrowed his brow as he tried to figure out what play Lou Stallings intended to make. He did not have to wait long to find out.

In a rush of sudden activity, Lou reached out with both hands and grasped his younger brother by the upper arms. Using his own weight, Lou spun Jacob, flinging him toward the army scout.

Levi Stout was ready for something, he just didn't know yet what it would be. When it came, his response was reflex. Stout swung the butt of his rifle at the hapless Jacob Stallings, catching the man square in the jaw with a heavy wooden stock. Jacob Stallings fell away. One hit was enough to put him on the ground. But he'd served the purpose that Lou set for him.

Now Lou Stallings flung open his coat, and his hand went for the six-shooter on his belt.

Stout shouted some warning not to do it, and Lou Stallings shouted back some curse as he wrenched the gun from its holster.

Stout swung the rifle back around, getting the barrel up before Stallings could clear leather. The cavalryman fired first, though his aim was off, his shot cutting through Lou Stallings' coat.

Stallings had the six-shooter free now, and thumbed back the hammer as he brought the thing level. Stout worked the lever, ejecting the spent casing, but he saw the six-shooter coming up and rolled away, trying to duck back into the woods. The gun in Lou Stallings' hand burst to life, and Stout felt the searing pain as the bullet cut through the sleeve of his coat and creased his muscle on his arm. He cursed the pain through gritted teeth, but he kept moving, and in a moment had disappeared into the trees.

Stallings fired a wild shot into the forest, and then another, shooting not at shadows or movement but at spaces where he thought Stout might have gone.

"Get your rifle!" Lou barked at his brother.

If Jacob felt any sense of animosity toward his brother for the rough use Lou put him to, he showed no sign of it. On hands and knees, Jacob scrambled over to the tent where he'd left his rifle. He snatched it up and then climbed to his feet.

"Where'd he go?" Jacob asked.

"In there somewhere," Lou said, and both men began to circle the camp, their guns directed into the woods.

Stout, meanwhile, limped back behind a pine tree and then dropped down into the ravine.

Stallings hit him with his first shot, just a grazing wound to his arm. But one of those wild shots fired into the woods had also hit him in the thigh.

The army scout gritted his teeth as he tried to examine the wound, though the gray dusk made it difficult to see anything. Using the knife on his belt, Stout cut a tear in his pants and reached his hand inside. He could feel the hole where the bullet entered his leg, and an exit wound around toward the back of his leg. It was painful as hell, but the bullet had gone straight through. There was no damage to the bone, and if he could get out of this alive, he might even heal without even a limp.

Stout crouched low and began working his way

through the ravine, past the body that until recently had belonged to Dicky Cort.

He wanted to get deep enough into the woods that when he came up from the ravine the Stallings brothers wouldn't see him.

Every step was painful, and he carried his arm tucked against his body. Though the arm was a smaller wound, to be sure, the pain in his arm seemed to be worse, even as he stepped down on the injured leg.

Ten, fifteen yards through the ravine, and Stout decided to chance it. He popped over the bank and crawled a few feet through the snow. The snow got into his cut britches, hit the wound, and the cold snow felt good against the gash in his leg.

Now he pushed himself up, and staying crouched, worked himself behind where the horses were picketed. Their movement would conceal his movement in the trees. He could see the Stallings brothers, both of them facing away from the camp, both of them with their guns up, both of them facing the woods. Their heads jerked this way and that, any noise or shadow that they thought they saw drawing their attention.

Stout raised up the rifle, painful as it was to lift his arm, and drew an aim on Lou Stallings. But even as he did, the man stepped so that he was behind a tree, and Stout lost the shot.

"There he is!" Jacob Stallings shouted, but he was facing the entirely wrong way. Now both men fired a couple of shots apiece into the woods at some unknown shadow.

"Did we hit him?" Lou said.

"I don't know," Jacob said. "I lost him."

Lou Stallings stepped forward, directly into the space where Levi Stout was aiming. The army scout squeezed his trigger, and the shot flew straight. He caught Lou Stallings just below the armpit on the left side. Before Lou even moved, Stout dropped the lever and fired another shot. This one hit near where the first one hit.

Lou Stallings plunged forward, dropping his gun. He reached up to grab hold of a tree and steady himself, and then he pitched forward into the snow.

"Lou!" Jacob Stallings yelled, stepping forward and reaching toward his brother.

Stout did not have a shot, but he pushed his way through the cedars and stepped into the clearing of the campsite beside a picketed horse.

Jacob Stallings swung around, trying to bring his rifle to bear, but Stout already had the aim. He fired a shot, dropped the lever and fired a second shot. Both shots hit Jacob Stallings in the chest, knocking the man back.

Stepping carefully and keeping the rifle aimed between the two Stallings brothers sprawled on the ground, Levi Stout stepped forward into the light and warmth of the campfire.

He kicked away Lou Stallings' six-shooter and then reached down and grabbed Jacob's rifle and tossed it into the woods.

Lou Stallings was dead.

Jacob Stallings choked on his own blood, his eyes wide.

"I reckon that's you done for," Stout said, leaning against a pine tree so that he did not have to put weight on his injured leg.

He stood over the man and watched him die. It took several minutes, but Jacob Stallings did not speak another word.

***

Levi Stout waited for Jacob Stallings to die before he walked over closer to the fire. He did not enjoy watching the man die, nor did he enjoy taking the man's life. But he stayed around in case there was an opportunity to do something for the man.

As he watched Jacob Stallings fight for his final breaths, the army scout reflected on the tremendous waste – so many men murdered and killed, all for greed. Stout found it hard to imagine what motivated men. He didn't have much, a cabin that needed constant repairs, a couple of good saddle horses in a barn, a small kitchen garden, and a good woman who waited for him to return home. But Stout couldn't think of a thing that could be bought with gold dust that was more valuable than the little he had, nor anything so valuable as a man's life.

But the Stallings brothers had been willing to trade every life they encountered for a producing mine.

"It's a damn, foolish waste," Stout said.

When Jacob Stallings was all finished up, Stout took on the burden he'd been avoiding.

Even in the few moments that he'd been in the camp, he'd seen the felled, rotting tree trunk all chewed to hell by lead bullets and guessed at what it must have meant. The tree trunk, combined with the pile of dead bodies, told Levi Stout that Lieutenant Turner had been here and there'd been a good fight. He doubted that the lieutenant would have left here with Jacob Stallings still alive.

Stout found the lieutenant on the other side of the rotting pine tree. He was half-buried in the snow that fell freely down through the opening of the canopy. Stout guessed the man had been there like this for maybe an hour or a little more.

Snow landed on the lieutenant's face, his unseeing eyes did not blink against the flakes.

One more sad waste, Stout thought.

He found a blanket to wrap the body in and pulled the lieutenant nearer to the campsite, though not too close to the campfire. Then he dragged the Stallings brothers out of the campsite and over to where Jacob Stallings had piled up the dead men from his outfit.

When all of this was finally done, Stout sat down on a camp stool near the fire and he slid off his britches. The air was miserably cold, but Stout wanted to get a good look at his injury. He flushed it with warm water and then poured onto the wound liberal amounts from a bottle of whiskey he'd found in one of the tents. He tied a bandanna around the wound. Then he tossed some branches onto the fire and stretched out near enough to it that he could feel its warmth.

The posse might possibly arrive overnight, but if O'Keefe made it to Del Norte, they would definitely be here by midmorning.

They would be disappointed. Most often, when a man joined a posse, he did so with the hope that he'd have a chance to gun down an outlaw. But there were no outlaws left in these mountains, at least not this night. The only job for the posse now would be to collect the dead, and none of them would be happy for that.

If O'Keefe didn't make it to Del Norte, no posse would be coming. Either way, Stout intended to stay here for the night. The fire was warm and there were supplies and provisions. If the posse turned up, he'd show them where to find the dead. They would leave those two he'd killed in the pass. Come morning, whether there was a posse or not, Stout would put the lieutenant's body on one of the horses, and he'd take another one, and he would ride out of here alone.

If he picked the right two horses, he could make Del Norte in two days. Another couple of days and he'd be back to Fort Garland to make his report. In a week, he would be home with Faustina. She would make a fuss over the injuries to his arm and leg, but she would be relieved to see him, and she would keep him warm and healthy through the winter.

EIGHT MONTHS LATER

- 44 -

Sergeant O'Keefe stepped lightly from the train to the platform at the depot, waiting to feel the wooden leg steady against the platform.

He was still trying to get accustomed to walking on a peg leg. His uniform, and the straps of the fake leg going across his thigh, drew some sympathetic stares, but O'Keefe ignored those. It had been some years since folks had grown so used to seeing a man in a uniform with a missing limb that they'd stopped staring. And though there were plenty of men around now in civilian clothes with sleeves pinned up or wooden legs strapped to stumps, O'Keefe's uniform seemed to be a novelty.

He had only a small satchel that he slung over his shoulder as he made his way along the platform. Out on the busy main road, he found a hack and gave the driver the address. A short while later, after a pleasant ride from the bustling old town and then past pleasant New England residences and well-maintained yards, O'Keefe found himself walking up a brick front walk to a large, brick house with big windows and painted shutters. It was mid-spring, now, and O'Keefe was on his way home to New York. Not entirely certain of what the future would hold for him, he had a pension and he looked forward to seeing his ma and pa.

He used his cane on the walk, though he was trying to get around without the cane.

"Are you Major Turner?" O'Keefe asked the gray-haired man at the door. O'Keefe had sent a telegram ahead to announce his intention for a visit.

"You must be Sergeant O'Keefe," the man said. He eyed the leg. "Please come in and have a seat."

"A fine lad he was," O'Keefe said, settling himself into the sofa. "He had the makings of an outstanding officer. And fearless, I can say that, as well."

The older man nodded his head. He seemed thoughtful.

"It's kind of you to come and see me like this," Major Turner said. "I appreciate knowing that he conducted himself commendably."

"Oh, that he did, sir. That he did. He turned back, you know. We were making for Del Norte, after the troopers had been killed, to raise a posse. But your nephew, Lieutenant Turner, he said he would go back to buy us time."

"And you were the only survivor?" Major Turner asked.

"Oh, no, sir. We had a scout with us, and he survived as well. He was the one who give me this to give to you." O'Keefe reached into his satchel and withdrew an old cap-and-ball Colt. "The lieutenant carried this. I believe he said it was his father's from the war, which I suppose makes it your brother's."

Major Turner took the pistol and looked at it.

"Sentimental," he said, holding up the old Colt. "That he would carry this."

"I reckon so, yes, sir."

O'Keefe had never been in a house so nice, and he found himself intimidated by the wealth. The older Turner's rank didn't much impress him. O'Keefe had little use for most officers, and the higher the rank the less impressed he was.

"Would you stay for dinner?" Major Turner asked, carefully placing his brother's gun on a table beside his chair.

"No, sir," O'Keefe said quickly. He nodded his head toward the front window. "No, I've got the hack waiting, and I should get back to the train station. I'm bound for New York to see my parents. It's been quite a while."

Turner nodded his head. He did not seem overly disappointed.

"It's good of you to come here," he said.

"He would have made a fine officer," O'Keefe said again.

As he used his cane to walk back down the brick walk to where the hack waited for him, O'Keefe wished that there was something more he could have said. And then he realized that wasn't it at all. Instead, he realized he wished he could have said it to someone different. He wished there'd been a girl to mourn for the young lieutenant, maybe a son to hand the pistol to. The lieutenant's uncle, O'Keefe decided, seemed too damned indifferent to the loss of his nephew.

In the hack on the way back to the train station, Paddy O'Keefe thought of the young lieutenant. None of it had been his fault, really. The scout, particularly, had cemented the lieutenant's reputation when he returned to Fort Garland. He'd talked of how the lieutenant had gone into the mountains to lure the Stallings outfit in the wrong direction. He'd given the lieutenant credit for killing a number of those men.

O'Keefe did not know what had occurred between Turner and Stout on those four days outside of Del Norte, but Turner clearly left the scout impressed.

For his part, Levi Stout returned to his wife and that winter moved her to Santa Fe with him. He quit the army altogether and took up a job riding shotgun on a stagecoach. Several times while O'Keefe convalesced at the hospital in Santa Fe, Stout came to see him. He never spent much time, but they'd sit and chat, and Stout would bring with him to the hospital some treat his wife baked.

And the day that Stout came and announced his wife was pregnant, he handed the cavalry sergeant a cigar.

"If it's a boy, I think I'll name him Turner."

His uncle might have been indifferent, but it occurred to O'Keefe that in those four days outside of Del Norte, Lieutenant Turner left a favorable impression on what remained of his command.

the end

ABOUT THE AUTHOR

Robert Peecher is the author of more than two score of Western novels. He is former journalist who spent 20 years working as a reporter and editor for daily and weekly newspapers in Georgia.

Together with his wife Jean, he's raised three fine boys and a mess of dogs. An avid outdoorsman who enjoys hiking trails and paddling rivers, Peecher's novels are inspired by a combination of his outdoor adventures, his fascination with American history, and his love of the one truly American genre of novel: The Western.

For more information and to keep up with his latest releases, we would encourage you to visit his website (mooncalfpress.com) and sign up for his twice-monthly e-newsletter.

OTHER NOVELS BY ROBERT PEECHER

THE LODERO WESTERNS: Two six-shooters and a black stallion. When Lodero makes a graveside vow to track down the mystery of his father's disappearance, it sends Lodero and Juan Carlos Baca on an epic quest through the American Southwest. Don't miss this great 4-book series!

THE TWO RIVERS STATION WESTERNS: Jack Bell refused to take the oath from the Yankees at Bennett Place. Instead, he stole a Union cavalry horse and started west toward a new life in Texas. There he built a town and raised a family, but he'll have to protect his way of life behind a Henry rifle and a Yankee Badge.

ANIMAS FORKS: Animas Forks, Colorado, is the largest city in west of the Mississippi (at 14,000 feet). The town has everything you could want in a Frontier Boomtown: cutthroats, ne'er-do-wells, whores, backshooters, drunks, thieves, and murderers. Come on home to Animas Forks in this fun, character-driven series.

TRULOCK'S POSSE: When the Garver gang guns down the town marshal, Deputy Jase Trulock must form a posse to chase down the Garvers before they reach the outlaw town of Profanity.

FIND THESE AND OTHER NOVELS BY ROBERT PEECHER AT AMAZON.COM

Made in the USA
Las Vegas, NV
02 November 2024